where those remaining members of the 100 Blades would await their fate.

King Willem and Queen Gwendolyn joined the Farrunners, with King William stating, "Let us go inside and give these young heroes a chance to wash and rest up before dinner tonight. Before we depart, please turn and give the wonderful people of our land another wave".

All in attendance, except for the four guards with the Farrunners, let out wide arcing waves to the crowd. One last eruption of cheers came so loud that it could be felt by all standing on the castle steps. The men and women of Terramilene continued to clap and cheer as the last member of the Cromwell's, and their guests, filed through Castle Brightstone's entry.

Chapter Two

A servant led Lucien, the twins, and Arissa upstairs. The long hallway led to individual rooms for the young guests. They all agreed they would see each other later for dinner. Lucien entered his room to find a royal attendant waiting to take care of his needs. There was a hot bath waiting for him. Lucien began to take his clothes off only to realize how bad they, and he, smelled. He had to laugh to himself as he realized that when on the road there isn't time for such luxuries as a bath. Everyone traveling in the group smells just as bad and the odors tend to blend. The best one can do on the road is perhaps a quick rinse in a cold stream and chew some peppermint but there wasn't time for that on the crusade Lucien and his friends had gone on. Without hesitation, Lucien dipped himself in the hot bath slowly enjoying every moment.

"I'll have these cleaned for you master Lucien. Is there anything you need now?" the royal attendant said as he picked up Lucien's dirty clothes.

"What is your name?" Lucien asked.

"Hanson, sir," the attendant replied.

"Hanson, thank you," Lucien said

"Very good sir. When you are finished bathing just ring that bell and I will bring you a robe," Hanson said.

"Thank you Hanson, but it may be a while. I am going to enjoy this bath until the water is cold." Lucien said.

"You are very welcome sir. And, if anyone deserves a long bath it is you. You've earned it and so much more," Hanson replied as he bowed and closed the door to the bathing room behind him.

Lucien closed his eyes and let the hot water seep into his muscles. After the heat from the water began to wane he went to task on scrubbing his body from head to toe, then he did it again to ensure nothing was missed. When he stood and looked at the murky water he had a quick laugh and a shake of his head. He rang the bell as directed, though it felt foreign to him, and Hanson came in carrying a fine cotton robe.

"If you don't mind sir, please stand here. I need to take measurements for our castle tailor as you will need new clothes for dinner," Hanson stated.

"I will? What's wrong with what I had on when I entered the bathing room? Are they not fine enough for dinner?" Lucien asked with a smirk that let Hanson know the questions was a joke.

Lucien stood on a small pedestal where Hanson took Lucien's measurements quickly and efficiently.

"If there is nothing else you need sir I will leave you to get some rest before dinner," the attendant said.

"That bed is all I need right now Hanson," Lucien replied.

"Very good sir. I will return in two hours' time, and I will bring you proper attire for dinner. It will *not* be those you arrived in," Hanson said, his own joke making the two smile.

Lucien laughed then finished with, "Thank you, Hanson. You have been too kind."

"You're welcome sir," Hanson replied and closed the door to Lucien's room.

Lucien sat on the edge of his bed waiting for a knock. The knock he had become accustomed to after his friends and he were placed in singular rooms. The knock that brought both joy and then confusion. Almost on the moment it was expected, the knock came. He was speaking as he opened the door, "I was waiting for you."

"Were you now?" Brienne asked.

"Brienne! I'm sorry I thought you were…"

"Arissa?" Brienne teased.

"Yes, Arissa," Lucien said.

"Well I'm sorry to disappoint you but I am here to tell you to not wait up for her. She will see you at dinner," Brienne said, clearly enjoying Lucien's embarrassment.

"Is everything alright?" Lucien asked.

"Everything is perfect cousin. Now get some rest, you have all earned it. I'll see you at dinner," Brienne said as she kissed Lucien's cheek, smiled and left.

Lucien was a little disappointed in the turn of events, but he couldn't give much energy to thinking of it. The bath had done its job well and relaxed his body. The huge bed seemed to know his name; he would swear he heard it calling to him. He leaped on it and his first, and last, thought was that the bed was so comfortable it must be the same if one was to lay upon a cloud.

"Come in," Lucien said with a scratchy voice. A knock on the door brought him out of a dreamless sleep.

Hanson entered with the clothes Lucien was to wear for dinner. Everything was fine silks and linens. There was a pair of calf-high boots that were beautiful but since they were not broken in they were a little uncomfortable. Lucien would never complain about that though. Hanson led Lucien out into the hallway where Rob and Tom were waiting. All three boys began laughing knowing just how different they all looked in these fancy clothes, combed hair, and a fresh shave for the twins.

"The lady Arissa will join us later. Gentlemen if you will, follow me," Hanson said as he led them to the dining hall where the two kings, Rory, William, and Quinn were waiting.

"Ah here they are Killian. They clean up well don't they?" King Willem said.

"You were right Willem they look like proper young men now. Come over here boys join us," King Killian said.

A servant came over to the boys with a tray with glasses of wine on it. Each boy took a glass and joined the group who had already started into their libations.

"I want you all to know that when we arrived here yesterday Queen Sera and I spoke with King Willem and Queen Gwendolyn and told them everything. From what I did to my brother to everything that happened to him, your mother Elena, Lucien, and everyone who went with him. I told him your story Lucien and everything that has befallen you. I begged their forgiveness for not sharing with them what happened with Brohm. I should have told them because they loved him too. I was bound by foolish pride and traditions that no longer serve a purpose. Then I was bound by my own shame. Their trust had been earned long ago and I should have known that anything I shared with them in secret would be safe with them," King Killian said. His face was filled with pain, but his voice was filled with conviction on the message he was sharing.

"And we told you there was nothing to forgive my friend. Your brother loved you and would not have you burdened by shame and guilt. Enough talk of regrets we are here to celebrate these young heroes," King Willem said as he swept his arm out to the boys, then continued with, "You should all get used to that title *young heroes* it's what the people are calling you. You have accomplished what we could not. King Killian and I had hunted the 100 Blades for a decade and now they are no more because of all of you."

King Willem raised his glass to the young men. King Killian and William raised their glasses as well.

"You have all brought great honor to your families. We couldn't be prouder," King Killian said.

The boys seemed anything but comfortable with all the attention. Even Quinn, who earlier reveled in the crowd's cheers, seemed oddly subdued with all this personal praise. There was nothing to do but put on a smile and consume the wine in unison with the toast makers.

"Ah here come the ladies," King Willem said.

Everyone looked to the top of the stairs. First came Queen Gwendolyn. It didn't seem possible, but she was more beautiful than ever. She wore a white silk dress and had her hair elaborately done in interweaving tight braids. A beautiful diamond necklace was around her neck, and she had beautiful diamond earrings, that bounced rainbow refracted light around her jawline and down her neck. It all made it seem as if there was a glow about her. When she reached the bottom of the stairs King Willem exclaimed how breathtaking she looked. He then took her hand and led her to the dinner table.

Queen Sera was next. So different from Queen Gwendolyn, but no less beautiful, wore a full-length green silk dress complimented with emerald necklace, bracelet and earrings. The color of green radiated off the backdrop of her darker skin complexion. King Killian met her at the bottom step and whispered something in her ear as they made their way to the table, which made her giggle and slap the king's arm playfully.

Next came Brienne looking every bit the princess she was. Covered in a dark blue dress that flared wide at her knees, sapphires pinned into the tight bun atop her head, a sapphire and diamond necklace made a wide v shape from her collar bones down to the center of her chest. She radiated the type of beauty only a young woman can. William met her at the bottom of the stairs, told his sister she looked lovely, kissed her cheek, and led her to the dinner table.

Then came Arissa. The five boys at the bottom of the stairs stared in stunned silence. She was barely recognizable. Her dress was a type of red, but Lucien didn't know the name of the color. All he knew was that it went perfectly with her pulled back hair and the rubies she was wearing around her neck. Simple but exquisite red earrings complimented her ears and a thin bracelet made of black stones stood out in contrast to all of the red. Lucien stood there in amazement. Quinn elbowed him in the ribs and Lucien hurried to the bottom of the stairs to wait for her.

"Arissa…..you look beautiful," Lucien managed to say with a stutter.

"Thank you Lucien. You look very handsome yourself. Shall we have dinner?" Arissa asked.

"Yes," Lucien replied as he led Arissa to her seat at the table.

King Cromwell looked at everyone at the table, nodded, and in unison everyone sat. Dinner was lighthearted. Lucien, the twins, and Arissa watched everyone carefully before starting each course. They weren't used to the different utensils and wanted to make sure they weren't the odd ones using a large fork when a small one was required for a plate of salad or flat spoon when a curved one was to be used for a bowl of bisque.

The young men and woman were astonished at how each course seemed to outdo the previous one. It had been a long time since the *young heroes* had eaten a quality meal, and for some in the group, never had they eaten foods as delectable as that served at the table, so they ate their fill. When the meal was over everyone moved to the area of the dining room where there was a large fireplace and many sofas and large comfortable chairs for everyone to lounge in. Wine and brandy was brought by servants and the conversations continued.

"Robert, Thomas, my son tells me that you two do a magnificent re-creation of the fight between Lucien and Kane. I know I can speak for all of us who have not seen it that we look forward to your performance. Before that, unfortunately, we have serious matters to discuss. Lucien were you able to find out who hired the 100 Blades?" King Cromwell asked.

The air in the giant room seemed to grow thick as the question was asked. All the good nature of the evening was sucked away with the King's request. Lucien stood and faced everyone.

"I questioned Kane's number two, Jackson Royce…. the vampire lords hired them," Lucien informed the group.

A few sharp intakes of breath were heard at the startling nature of this news.

"Are you sure he was being truthful?" Prince William asked.

"Royce said the vampire lords hired them and all my senses said he spoke true. Their master mage, Malachi, said the reason why was because of some vague prophecy where a half-breed of human and wolf will thwart the vampires somehow. He kept his scent masked from me but Arissa and I both believe he most assuredly withheld information. During the battle, the mage was the only one to escape, so I was not able to question him further," Lucien said.

"Do you think this mage knew who you were?" asked King Killian.

"Hard to say uncle. I gave him a false name and false story as to how I came to be there in their *hidden* camp. My sense is that this mage is intelligent and cunning. As well as I believe I told this false story I am not used to lying and one such as he may have picked up on that. Or he may simply think that I too was not telling him everything. I simply do not know," Lucien replied.

"The implications are that the vampires are doing something that Lucien will interfere with," Rory added.

"But what?" Queen Gwendolyn said.

"I suggest we reconvene to discuss these matters after the Great Wood gets a chance to celebrate these young heroes," King Killian said.

At the king's word a look went through all of said heroes.

"I saw that. What are all of you hiding?" Queen Sera asked.

"About the celebration uncle," Lucien said.

"Yes what about it? Out with it Lucien," King Killian demanded.

"Uncle, do you remember when I told you about my time spent in captivity in Kabaal?" Lucien asked.

"Of course. King Cromwell and I have been thinking of ways to make them pay for that," King Killian replied.

"I told you of Master Stein and his amazing story. I gave him my word that if I survived my own quest I would look for his son and if I found him, that I would return to Kabaal, help him escape and reunite them," Lucien shared.

"Oh Lucien we just got you all back safe and sound from one dangerous situation, and now you want to run off into another?" Queen Sera asked.

"Aunt Sera I am sorry, but I gave my word. Dr. Stein was good to me, and he has been enslaved by a tyrant for over a century. He is a good and brilliant man who should not be held captive any longer. I believe his son to be two days west of Terramilene. There is a town called Stormville at the foot of a mountain called Stormmount. It is there on that mountain that I believe I will find his son Derian. He's been alone for over 100 years thinking his father abandoned him. It isn't right and I swore to help," Lucien said.

"I suppose you'll be going as well Quinn?" Queen Sera asked with a not-so-subtle raise of her eyebrows.

"Yes mother," Quinn replied quietly.

"When will you be leaving?" Brienne asked.

"Tomorrow morning," Lucien replied.

"So soon! You need time to prepare for such a journey," Queen Sera said.

"I had Lucien tell the quartermaster all that he would need for the journey. I received word just before dinner that all that he needed would be waiting for him at the western gate in the morning," Rory said.

"Did you now Rory?" King Cromwell asked, his eyebrows mimicking that of Queen Sera.

"Yes father. My brothers and sister needed me, and I will always answer that call," Rory replied as he looked his father in the eyes. It was the first time he was standing on his own feet in making a decision with such implications.

"I would expect nothing less, after all we are all family here," King Willem said.

"Well, I can't have the Cromwell's taking all the credit for this journey. There must be something else you need Lucien," King Killian said.

"Yes uncle there is," Lucien replied.

"Name it"

"We need two more wolves to volunteer to accompany us. When we make our escape from the city of Oasis we will need them to run the desert of Kabaal with riders on their backs. Whichever two you choose can track and catch up to us long before we reach Kabaal," Lucien informed his uncle, and the table of the plan.

"While I'm sure the list of volunteers to accompany you on your rescue mission would be long, I think I can do better than that. Timber, Benagar!" King Killian called.

"Yes my king," the two legendary guardsmen stepped forward and replied.

Lucien realized that he had not noticed the two guards all evening, yet they were obviously close by. He could think of no other word to describe their ability to meld into the environment than incredible.

"My son, my nephew, and their companions, need two more wolves to join them on their rescue mission. I would like those two wolves to be you two," King Killian said.

"Our place is beside the king your highness," Timber replied.

"Your place is where your king needs you to be. Besides how will those two you brought with you know what it feels like to guard the king if you don't let them guard the king?" Killian asked.

"They are not ready," Benagar replied.

"Ha! Ha! In your eyes Gar, no one will ever be ready. You both remember our wild reckless youth. Foolishly rushing into danger. I want you to go with them. Give them your wisdom. Make sure they don't make the mistakes we did. When I married Sera and started a family my adventuring days ended. You two became my most trusted guardsmen and also gave up your adventuring days. Consider this a gift from a grateful king and a grateful friend. Have another adventure while watching over my family. Please don't make me order you to," King Killian said.

Both guardsmen took in and let out a deep breath, "Very well my king. We will go," Timber said.

"Uncle I don't know what to say. Thank you and thank both of you," Lucien said to the king and his guardsmen.

Benagar stepped up to Lucien, towered over him and said, "Just because this mission is yours Lucien doesn't mean you'll be ordering me and Timber around."

"I....I would never....," Lucien stammered.

"And that goes for you too Prince Quinn!" Benagar shouted.

"Wouldn't dream of it old bull!" Quinn replied. He then looked over to the twins and gave a quick smile and head nod indicating that he definitely dreamt of ordering the two new-comers around as much as possible.

"Methinks the prince will be paying for that old comment somewhere along the road. We will be at your disposal Lucien and will only take over if we feel you are leading us all to our deaths," Timber said.

"Thank you?" Lucien replied as Timber smiled and shook his hand.

The conversations came to an end and the King noted that he would expect the re-enactment of Lucien's battle as soon as this new quest was completed. He then bade all a goodnight. Everyone understood the evening was over, everyone lazily making their way to their rooms.

The knock on Lucien's door was from Arissa but unlike other nights the two only slept together. She didn't say anything to him as she found the perfect spot in the crease of his arm and leaning into his ribs. While the nights spent exploring each other's bodies was an unbelievable feeling, it was the feeling of her next to him when they woke up that brought a different feeling, a different satisfaction, but no less pleasing.

Chapter Three

The companions awoke early and made their way to the western gate of Terramilene where their supplies and both royal families were waiting to see them off. Firm handshakes, warm smiles, and wishes of safe travel were given from the more reserved king and queen of Terramilene, big hugs and cheek kisses from the Farrunners.

When Lucien reached his aunt she took his face in her hands, shook it playfully and said, "This is becoming a habit I don't like, watching my family go off on dangerous journeys while I wait nervously for you all to return."

"I know Aunt Sera. I'm sorry," Lucien said.

"No Lucien I am sorry. I should not have added to the weight of responsibility already on your shoulders with the words I spoke last night. It was just a mother's selfishness. You are keeping your word to your friend and hopefully reuniting him with his son. It is the right thing to do. Keep watch over each other, stay safe, and hurry home," Queen Sera said, then kissed him on the cheek.

Lucien turned away from his aunt to find his smiling Uncle Killian awaiting him.

"Don't worry about your aunt Lucien, she's strong. William, Brienne, and I will be with her, and we will strengthen each other as always," Killian said.

"It breaks my heart to know that I am causing her pain," Lucien said.

"She would never hold it against you Lucien. The situation is what it is. You all wouldn't be heroes without honor. I hate seeing you all leave again but you gave your word, and you must keep your word, always. When you reunite Master Stein with his son let them know that the king of the Great Wood welcomes them and, if they wish, they will have a home with us," the king shared.

"I will uncle," Lucien replied.

The king took a half step forward, looking Lucien purposely in the eyes, and said, "I'm proud of you Lucien." The look and tone was almost identical of Lucien's father when he would give words of encouragement or praise.

"Take advantage of these two," the king said as he pointed to Timber and Benagar standing before the two younger guardsmen who would be taking their place protecting the king while they were gone. From the looks of it Benagar was really giving it to them, while Timber just stared at them. Lucien didn't know which one was more frightening. To the two young guardsmen's credit they stood there perfectly still and just took it. No smell of fear came from them, only resolve.

"They both have much to offer. Listen to them. Ask them questions, you'll all be better for it. They have seen and done much, and they are warriors still," the king said.

"Thank you uncle I will," Lucien replied.

When his uncle was done embracing him, Lucien joined his friends who were standing with Rory. The entire group giving off a smell of anxiousness.

"I'm really tired of getting left behind. I have to stay and help process the 100 Blades prisoners. The records we seized tells all the specific crimes for each member. There will be a hanging each day for over a month. Take care of each other and hurry back. If you're not back in a month I'll be on the road the next day looking for you with the Legion," Rory said.

With that they all group hugged and began climbing into the two huge wagons. Lucien asked for horses built for strength and the sturdiest wagons that could be found. The quartermaster didn't disappoint and upon quick inspection everything Lucien asked for as far as supplies was accounted for and dispersed evenly between the two wagons. It bothered Lucien that one of the wagons and horse teams would be left behind in Kabaal, but there was simply no avoiding it.

Lucien offered his hand to Arissa as she climbed into the wagon. She sat next to him as he took the reins. When settled she looked over her shoulder to see Benagar and Timber on the bench behind her. Their bodies, and eyes, set stoically, ready for whatever this mission would bring. Quinn took up the reins of the other wagon while the twins mounted their own horses. The idea being the boys could pretend to be guardsmen hired to help protect their caravan if need be and they can scout ahead on the road and move much more quickly than the horse teams again if need be. For now they took up positions on either side of Quinn's wagon.

With a final wave goodbye, the procession left Terramilene on their way to Stormville, and hopefully something more. As Lucien looked back he noticed Brienne and Rory standing very close together. There was something about the way they were standing. The wind was blowing the wrong way so he couldn't smell them, but even without the smell he knew something was going on.

After a couple of hours, if not more, of riding, Lucien finally couldn't hold it in any longer.

"Hey Quinn!" Lucien called to his cousin.

"Yes Lucien," Quinn replied.

"Did you notice something different about Brienne and Rory?" Lucien asked.

"You mean the way they were standing together when we left?" Quinn replied.

"Yes! I knew I was picking up on something!" Lucien said.

"Yes it was subtle almost as if they themselves didn't realize it," Quinn said.

Lucien felt Arissa tense, just a little. He gave a side glance to her, raised his eyebrows that conveyed he was suspicious and asked. "Arissa do you know something?"

"I know that if you two don't stop asking questions about things that are none of your business you each will be getting a rap on the nose from one of my arrows," Arissa said.

Rob and Tom laughed at that response and both twins agreed that Lucien and Quinn should stop their line of questioning.

"You both need to stop your laughing. I've got something for the both of you too," Arissa warned.

Silence was returned.

"If you ladies are done gossiping, can we eat lunch now?" Benagar asked.

Everyone chuckled at the surly question from the older wolf in the back of Lucien's wagon. They all enjoyed a light lunch of fruit while riding underneath a beautiful clear sky. The lands west of Terramilene were mostly wheat fields. Farmers toiled during harvest time to bring in the wheat for most of Arborreah. The wheat was high now and would be harvested soon. For now, it was a beautiful golden sea as the wind blew and gave the illusion of waves. The companions ate their lunch in pleasant silence as they enjoyed the day and the beauty of the land.

"Timber do you mind if I ask you a question?" Arissa said after finishing the last bites of her food.

"Young lady you may ask me anything," Timber replied.

"The king spoke about the three of you being wild in your youth. What exactly did he mean by that?" Arissa asked

Both Timber and Benagar chuckled at this question. She didn't show it, but Arissa was shocked they both showed any type of levity.

"Well young lady King Killian, Benagar, and I, along with a few others used to run all over Arborreah looking for trouble. We would go to Terramilene or anywhere for that matter that had a bar or an inn, drink too much, get into fights and laugh while doing it. When there were bandits or thieves that needed hunting we were the first to volunteer to hunt them. We were young and thought we were invincible. Even after Killian became king we all still ran wild," Timber said.

"Did my father run with you?" Lucien asked.

"No, he was just too young to be doing what we were doing. More than once he tried following us, trying to stay out of our scent and running well behind us, but we always caught him and wouldn't allow it," Timber replied.

"So, when did you stop?" Arissa asked.

"Well two things happened. The first I won't speak of on a beautiful day such as this, but the second was Killian met Sera. She was the best thing that ever happened to him. She told him the things that we as his best friends should have. That as a king he had responsibilities. That he couldn't go running off into danger whenever he wanted to. That he had to be around to rule his people. When Killian told Gar and I that his adventuring days were over it was an easy decision for us to tell him that we were going to be his personal guard and that he didn't have a choice in the matter," Timber said with a chuckle. "Does that answer your question young lady?"

"Yes thank you Timber," Arissa said.

"I would like to hear the story of the first thing that happened someday," Lucien said

"Perhaps someday I will tell you Lucien," Timber replied.

Benagar interrupted the trip down memory lane and asked, "I would very much like to know how you defeated Kane Lucien."

"I think I can do better than that. The twins performed the fight between Kane and I perfectly. Every move, every word, for Prince Rory and some of his men one night on the road back to Terramilene. I'm sure we can get them to do a repeat performance tonight after dinner," Lucien said.

"I look forward to it," Benagar replied.

The rest of the ride that day, and into the evening, Benagar didn't speak another word.

Just before it became too dark to continue riding, the group stopped and made camp in a clearing on the side of the road. After dinner, without much prodding, Rob and Tom re-enacted the fight between Lucien and Kane. The fire warming them only enhanced the intensity of the play. All in attendance gave a rousing round of applause to the two young men for their performance. Even Gar clapped with purpose.

"An amazing display young. I can see the both of you are formidable in your own right," Timber said.

"Thank you," the twins replied.

"That was a fantastic display of skill, but Lucien I would know what was in your mind, what you felt as you stepped onto the killing floor with an opponent such as Kane," Benagar asked.

Lucien took some time in thought before answering. When he spoke, he wanted to also share some of what he, and the others went through during their training.

Lucien started, "Master Kai Shen, the master of hand-to-hand combat, taught us that a true martial artist seeks that perfect blending of mind, body, and spirit. Believe it or not the physical part is the easiest. He taught us meditation and ways to strengthen the mind, and most important of all he taught us how to focus. How to take your emotions and make them work for you, not against you."

"Makes sense," Benagar said.

Lucien continued, "Uncontrolled emotion is the enemy going into a fight. It makes you sloppy and prone to mistakes. He taught us to focus on a flame in our mind's eye. Like this campfire. It is built to serve us. Cook our food, give us warmth, light, frighten away predators. If it was built poorly or left unattended then you may find yourself and all around you burned. I think that I can speak for all of us who went through training with Master Kai Shen when I say these skills have served us well."

"I'd say more than well," Timber added.

Lucien gave a quick laugh and started again with his dialogue, "I know I can see that focus on Arissa when she makes a shot that seems impossible. I can see it in Rob and

Tom. Master Stone said when the two of you fight together it is like the whirlwind and I agree."

Then Lucien looked directly at the large guardsman and said, "To answer your question Benagar, I took all that I was feeling before I stepped onto that killing floor and put it into that flame in my mind. Fear about what might happen to my friends if I were to lose. Feelings of anger and vengeance as I looked across at the man who led the attack on my village and killed my family. Any fear I felt for myself personally, well you can't have that either. If you go into a fight already afraid of your opponent, you are half-way beaten. I respected Kane's reputation, I knew this would be the fight of my life, obviously, so I put all those things into the flame, took a breath, and stepped onto the killing floor."

"He tried to break my focus with the things he said. He tried to rattle me by using those steel jackets he put on his fists. Master Kai Shen's training kept my focus unbroken. All I had to do after that was enact my strategy and trust that it would work. I trusted that like any fighter, especially one as skilled as Kane, would have my reach measured after the first few engagements. So, when I decided that the time was right to gamble on my strategy I narrowed my focus to a candle flame, called on the power of the wolf, and engaged Kane for what I hoped would be the last time. I knew I would only get one chance and then *my* surprise would be revealed."

"When I came across with my left at his mid-section he moved back with what he thought was enough room to avoid the strike, but he didn't account for the three inches of claw I extended at just the right moment. When I opened his belly, I knew he was done. Then the tiny little flame became a wildfire and the emotions I'd held in check came flooding in. Feelings of victory. Feelings of pride in killing a man that all said couldn't even be hit. Feelings of my friends being safe. Feelings of disbelief in the entire situation. The biggest emotion, and the one that set all of this into motion, was that maybe now the spirits of my parents and people could rest a little easier," Lucien said.

Lucien could feel Rob and Tom staring at him. He could feel their love for him. Arissa took his hand and squeezed it. This is the first time he had spoken of his feelings surrounding his fight with Kane. He didn't even know he needed to talk about it until this moment and he was thankful for Benagar's question.

In a rather somber tone, Lucien asked, "I hope this answers your question Gar."

"It does young Lucien. Could I trouble you with one more question?" Benagar asked.

"Of course, and there is no trouble at all," Lucien replied.

"Do you have those things Kane wore on his fists with you now?"

"Yes, they are in my pack,"

"May I see them?"

Lucien pulled his pack out and started rummaging through it.

"I am a student of combat and am always interested in new weapons," Benagar told the group as Lucien was looking for the weapons.

"Here you are Benagar," Lucien said.

Benagar took the weapons from Lucien and began to study them carefully.

"Such a simple design but I can see them being used to devastating effect," Benagar said as he handed them back to Lucien

"When we return to the Great Wood may I borrow them. I would like to have a blacksmith make me a pair," Benagar asked

"Of course," Lucien replied.

Instead of erecting tents, everyone slept under the wagons as the night air was so nice and comfortable. Timber set up a rotating watch but only woke Benagar well after half the evening had passed. Benagar allowed the young ones to sleep the rest of the twilight away. Some conversations about everyone being able to carry their weight went onto deaf ears of the two elder warriors.

The next day was as beautiful as the one before. By midday they could see the mountains before them and one particular peak showed storm clouds gathering around it, which marked their destination. If travel stayed as steady and unimpeded, the caravan would arrive the next evening, a little before dinnertime.

"So, Lucien, what can we expect?" Timber asked after they had made camp for the second evening.

"As far as the town, I'm not sure. I know nothing of it. If Derian is in the area that means he has been living there for almost one hundred years. It stands to reason they live together, Derian and the town, in some sort of unspoken agreement to leave each other alone and unharmed. We will find out when we arrive in the town. As far as Derian goes he has been living in relative solitude for all that time, thinking his father left him. He has been met with scorn and outright fear due to his startling size. His father said he is intelligent, inquisitive, and has a gentle heart. I would think if he harmed anyone he would have been hunted down regardless of his size. I hope one hundred years of solitude has not hardened him. If we do find him please control your reaction to the sight of him. I'm going to call him by his name and tell him his father sent us to find him and hopefully that will keep him calm even though we may be the first people he has seen face to face in a long time," Lucien said.

"You feel sorry for him, don't you Lucien?" Quinn asked.

"I do. Take a moment, all of you, and just think what it would be like to wake up one day and the one person you had in all the world was gone. No letter left behind, no explanation, just gone. And when you went out into a world you didn't really know wanting someone, anyone to help you, all you were met with was scorn, derision, and fear. When I began my journey after my family was killed I didn't know the world either. I met some terrible people along the way, but I would like to say I met far more who were willing to help. Compared to Derian's journey I was lucky," Lucien said.

"It is a sad tale Lucien. I think I can speak for all of us when I say we will help you make it a happier story," Tom said.

"Aye," everyone replied in unison.

When they all turned in that night, again sleeping under the wagons, Rob demanded to take the first watch. All the young travelers agreed they would not go another night not taking a watch, even if that meant never waking Timber or Gar.

As everyone made their way to their patch of grass Arissa crawled in next to Lucien, leaned in close to him and whispered in his ear, "You are a good man Lucien Farrunner."

Lucien pulled her close, kissed her forehead and they fell asleep together.

Chapter Four

The travelers arrived at the outskirts of Stormville where a beautifully hand-painted sign greeted them that read: *Welcome to Stormville home of the legendary Stormmount Giant. Inquire about tours at the Lightning Rod Inn.*

"Well, that's interesting," Tom said.

"I guess we go to the inn then," said Lucien.

Stormville was a very large town and surprisingly clean considering the amount of rainfall it endured. The people of Stormville devised an impressive irrigation and runoff system that kept the streets dry. As the caravan of Lucien and his group steered their wagons into town they were greeted with friendly head nods and pleasant waves. The Lightning Rod Inn was easily the biggest building in town, and would stand out as large in almost any town it would be in. A large stable on the side of the inn was more than enough room for all twelve of the horses and both wagons. After the stable boys were instructed to watch their wagons and take care of the horses, and after they were sufficiently terrorized by Benagar as to what horrible consequences there would be if anything went missing or the horses were NOT taken care of, the companions finally left the stable.

Entering the Lightning Rod Inn was the same as most inn's but triple the size. Three long tables, that could easily sit a dozen individuals on each side, were in the center of the room. Many smaller tables in varying sizes sat on the sides and a long bar was found at the opposite end of the entrance.

While the companions didn't eat terrible by any stretch of the imagination, all of their stomachs groaned with pleasure as the smells wafting from the kitchen were fantastic.

Surprising to all of them, the patrons already in the dining area gave smiles of welcome instead of looks of suspicion.

"Welcome friends, find any table that's available and I'll be there to serve you shortly," A woman with a bright face and brighter eyes said from across the room.

Arissa spotted a table not far from the entrance that would seat the entire group. It must have been a sight for the individuals engaged in eating and drinking as the travelers unloaded their weapons and gear. The twins leaned their staves in the corner behind their table. Arissa placed her bow in front of the staves. Lucien wasn't paying attention to the strap on his harness and almost dropped his swords. Quickly he sat down, leaned his swords against his chair and did his best not to let his red cheeks be seen by anyone.

"I think we are a little *overdressed*. If you know what I'm saying," Tom said to the table.

Those at the table with the ability of scent knew there was no danger amongst all the people in that large room. They shared that information with the others, and it appeared the town was as friendly as it seemed.

"Possibly true brother, but even after Gar's threats to those stableboys are you willing to leave your stave in the wagon? I'm not," Rob said.

All knew how valuable their weapons were. It isn't each day someone receives a stave, bow or sword infused with magic. They were too valuable to let out of their sight even if it meant being out of place in a room full of peaceful people. Timber and Benagar didn't remove their short swords and they didn't care what it looked like or how others might react to it.

"Welcome to the Lightning Rod Inn. You all look like you are ready to eat and have at least two, maybe three, pints. Our ale is very popular, and for good reason, but if you don't mind me saying it, our mead is the best there is. Of course we have choice wines and for those of you looking for something a little stronger I know we have some mash that has been approved by all the burly woodsmen," The waitress shared.

"What's cooking in the kitchen? It smells delicious," asked the twins.

"Today's special we have roasted beef that has been braised in a sweet honey sauce, served with potatoes and mixed greens. There is also warmed bread with an aged soft cheese for three pence. If you get two of those I'll only charge five pence," the waitress replied.

The table agreed on the bread as well as the meat, ordering two whole roasts, and enough sides for everyone and ale to go around. Arissa asked to try the mead.

"I'll bring the ales, and the mead for the beautiful young woman, while your food is prepared," the waitress said while throwing a wink at the twins, which left both thinking that wink was for one and not the other.

Their waitress returned with another waitress in tow, carrying all the mugs of ales and a small goblet for the mead. The new waitress, who was just as young and pretty as the first waitress, smiled at the twins as she walked away, each one again thinking the smile was just for them personally.

While they waited for their food, the group drank their libations, which was cold and delicious, and simply watched and listened to the people in the room. About twenty minutes later the two waitresses, and a servant boy, brought out the food. It was a spectacle that the entire dining area enjoyed watching. Whispers and smiles were given as plate after plate landed on the table of the newest set of travelers to patron the Lightning Rod Inn. The group didn't care about the wondering eyes as they were very hungry and ate their fill of the delicious meal.

As the waitresses were taking away the empty plates, Lucien asked the original waitress, "Excuse me miss?"

"Yes sir," she replied.

"Could you send for the person who runs the mountain tours? My friends and I would like to go on one," Lucien said.

"Of course sir," she replied.

"And another round of ale please," Quinn said.

"And a mead!" Arissa said a little too loudly.

The waitress smiled at her and said, "I told you they were delicious. Be careful though, they can sneak up on you."

"Nothing is sneaking up on me…" Arissa started but realized she was already feeling the effects and needed to stop talking.

"Another round of drinks and the guide coming up," the waitress said as she walked back toward the bar.

A few minutes later the waitresses returned with their fresh drinks and a smiling young man.

"Welcome to Stormville gentleman and lady. I hear you would like a mountain tour," the man said.

"Yes. Please, join us," Lucien requested.

As the man grabbed an empty chair from an adjoining table the twins and Quinn slid their chairs over, making room for the guide to sit next to Lucien.

"My name is James Lattimore, and I indeed run the tours. Actually, you are in luck. Tomorrow night a storm is rolling in, a real thundercracker, and the giant is sure to be out and bellowing," he said.

"What do you mean?" Lucien asked.

"Whenever there is a storm, which is quite often, hence the town and the mountains name, you can clearly hear the giant bellowing," James said.

Lucien leaned close to James, slid him a gold coin, and said, "James, my friends and I are interested in the real history of the giant. We know the story of the town's initial contact with the giant. How he took things here and there. How the townspeople confronted him, and he frightened them off, saying he just wanted to be left alone. We want to know the history from after that encounter until now. No detail is too small. We want to know everything even what you may not tell the tourists."

James thought about the request for a moment, looked around the table to see all eyes set on him were serious in the request and replied simply with, "Alright."

"This is the history as I know it. My ancestor was one of the original townspeople to confront the giant. After that original encounter, things just went on as usual. The giant would come down from the mountain and, as you mentioned, take a few things. Never too much and he never hurt anyone. So, the town grew comfortable with the way things were. It has been said that we Lattimores are too curious and stubborn for our own good. My ancestor decided that he will go alone and try to talk to the giant. The townspeople were against the idea. They didn't want any trouble from the giant and thought going up to the giant alone would bring just that. But, like I said, stubborn and off he went to try again.

Two days went past, and my ancestor had not returned, and the town assumed that the giant killed him. The town may have feared the giant, but they were no cowards and the murder of one of their own could not go unpunished. This time instead of a small group going to see the giant, the town gathered every able-bodied man and armed themselves. They were just going to go up the mountain when here came my ancestor walking down the mountain just as unharmed as when he left."

"The town was amazed and of course wanted to know everything about the last two days he spent with the giant. He told them how he convinced the giant that he meant no harm. How he was by himself and unarmed. The giant was not happy at first but for whatever reason he invited him into his cave and for the next two days they stayed up talking. He told them the giant was polite and highly intelligent. The giant told him nothing of his past and wouldn't even tell him his name. He told the townspeople that he felt a sadness from the giant. He said that the giant meant them no harm but that he still didn't want anyone disturbing his privacy. The giant told him that he alone would be allowed past the established border. So, my ancestor came down from the mountain with two things that day, an amazing story, and ideas."

"During their initial talk my ancestor said in passing how the frequent rainfall and runoff from the mountain made the streets horribly muddy. The giant told my ancestor that on his next visit to bring paper and something to write with. After my ancestor came down after his second visit with the giant he had the beginning plans to the irrigation and runoff system that you see around town today. This system completely changed our town for the better. The streets were dry, and it turned out that this system could be used for the surrounding wheat farms. The wealth from selling this system to the local farmers further transformed this town into something better for all who lived here."

"It wasn't long before this area became the primary wheat supplier for most of Arborreah. They obviously kept the giant's part in this a secret. The townspeople were grateful for what he had given them, so they respected his wishes for privacy."

"My ancestor on one trip tried to give the giant a share in the profits the town was making, but he wasn't interested in money, and told my ancestor to give his share back to the town. My ancestor asked him if he wanted anything. The giant told him that the town could give him things like they always have. He especially wanted books. Books on any subject. The townspeople did just that. They even purchased books for him. The townswomen would bake him pies, the men would leave him tools, and Stormville blossomed, and the town and the giant lived in content harmony."

"But the giant doesn't age or if he does it is so slow as to not be noticed. My ancestor did age and when he knew it was it was going to be the last time he would be able to make the trip up the mountain for one more visit he asked the giant if he wanted anyone else to take his spot and come visit him. The giant told my ancestor that he knew this day would come. He had grown fond of my ancestor and his visits, and he would mourn his passing, but he did not want to go through that again, so no he didn't want anyone going past the boundary anymore. He wanted to be left alone again."

"Things went back to the way they were in the beginning, and no one bothered the giant again. It had become known by this time about the giant's ritual of when the storm comes the giant would bellow with the storm. So, my great-grandfather had an idea. He wanted to lead people to the boundary of the giant's land during a storm so you could hear for yourself the Giant of Stormville. After his first tour, word got out that you could hear the bellow of the legendary Giant of Stormville. Turns out people like to be scared, safely mind you. People just kept coming. My great-great grandfather started charging a fee for the tours and people stayed at the inn, which was much smaller at the time. The inn had to expand to accommodate so many visitors to the size it is today. People spent their time and money here and Stormville continued to prosper," James said.

"Sounds like your great-great grandfather had a good mind for business," Timber said.

"My grandfather and father both said he was very smart. Anyway, the business of the tours got handed down to me and here we are," James said.

"Have you ever heard the giant bellow?" Lucien asked.

"I have. Many times," James replied.

"Please tell me what it is like," Lucien said.

At that question the table saw James's face change. He went from an upbeat storyteller and salesman to a man who was thoughtful about his answer.

"I will describe it as best I can. There is sadness in it, but not always. Sometimes it seems he bellows with the storm as if he is a part of it. As if there is a relationship between the two. It is hard to describe but that's the best way I can think to describe it," James said.

"Has no one ever tried, since the time of your ancestor, to go beyond the border and talk to him?" Arissa asked.

"Things have been this way for a long time miss. Things stay a certain way for a long time and it just becomes the way it is. Fear is a very small part of it, as I said he's never hurt anyone. People do fear change though. I think the town fears a change in the arrangement we have always had with the giant if we disrespect his wish to be left alone. I think many people think of him as a sort of lucky charm."

"We owe our prosperity to him, so we leave him alone and give him what gifts we can. As far as outsiders go, legends are a funny thing. There will always be those who do not believe and wish to disprove said legend. The few who have come along over the years who wished to disprove our legend, well there is something else that has been said about us Lattimores. We're good talkers, and we've always been able to put enough doubt in the hearts of those who have wished to cross the giant's boundary to turn away from such a foolish idea or face the giant's wrath," James said while making a comically scary face.

The table gave a gracious laugh at his attempt at humor, but none sitting there were in the mood to be entertained.

"Thank you very much James," Lucien said.

"It was my pleasure. So the next tour will leave from here tomorrow after sundown. We provide raincloaks and lanterns. It's about an hour's walk to the giant's border in the rain," James said.

"We'll see you tomorrow night James," Lucien said.

After James left Lucien looked at the table and asked, "Thoughts?"

"He never lied once through that entire story," Benagar said.

"I believe the giant is trying to protect his heart from feeling anymore loss. I've seen it before. The fact that he wanted no one else to visit him after James's ancestor's death tells me this," Arissa said.

"I agree young Arissa. This would worry me if not for the fact that he bellows with the storm. Someone who tries to erase feelings from themselves, even loss, run the risk of becoming emotionless, even heartless. But these trips into the storm of his, though sometimes painful, let's us know that he does indeed still feel," Timber said.

"I'm just glad that he is here. Lucien the first part of this quest will be fulfilled tomorrow night," Rob said.

"You're right Rob, thanks for reminding me," Lucien said.

"I'm going to see about rooms for the night," Quinn said.

"I half expected to come here and find out that it was nothing but a legend or that he was no longer here, but he is and tomorrow night we'll find him," Lucien said.

"Everything will work out young Lucien," Benagar said.

"I hope so," Lucien replied.

Quinn returned to the table with keys with numbers attached to them. "They only had four rooms. Here's a room for the twins, here's a room for the elderly couple," this produced a growl from both Timber and Benagar, "And this key is for you and Arissa, Lucien. I took the last room for myself although I may not be in it by myself for very long if the looks from the waitresses I received are any indication," Quinn said with a smile.

"Hey they were looking at me!" the twins shouted in unison while pointing a finger at themselves. They then immediately turned to each other and said, "Hey!"

Arissa and Lucien went to their room as did Timber and Benagar. Lucien sat on the edge of the bed deep in thought.

"What's troubling you?" Arissa asked.

"I just want things to go well with Derian. I see so many similarities between his story and mine. The difference is I've got all of you to lean on and help me. He's been alone for almost a century. I cannot imagine how lonely he has been," Lucien said.

Arissa sat down beside him on the bed and said, "Lucien tomorrow is going to work out fine. We will find Derian and let him know he is not alone anymore. We will reunite him with his father. Now no more worrying. If you haven't noticed, I'm a little tipsy from the mead, we have our own room, and I for one am not going to waste it. We may not get another chance to be alone again for awhile," Arissa said with a playful smile.

The thought of not being alone with Arissa for awhile snapped Lucien out of his brooding. Even more so as Arissa stepped back from him and started undoing her shirt until it fell to the floor, leaving her bare chested and waiting for him to join her.

After Lucien and Arissa were finished making love, twice, they exchanged the always present statement of "still friends" before Arissa fell asleep. Lucien remembered when those two words confused him, now he welcomed them. Those two words had become he and Arissa's special thing. Their feelings had grown so much, they and everyone else knew it. Lucien knew that in time those two words would change and become three.

Chapter Five

The next day the companions walked around the town of Stormville merely enjoying the day until it was time for the tour. Just after they finished another wonderful meal, heavy stormclouds rolled in full of thunder and lightning. James came and gathered them at the appointed time for the tour. He took them behind the inn where raincloaks and lanterns were given to all. There were three other people taking the tour, a young couple with their young son. They were very excited to be going on the tour. With a smile, James began leading them up the mountain.

There was a clear path which made the trek easy going. James had to speak up to be heard over the storm. He was telling the whole group how the weather was perfect, and they were sure to hear the giant this night. About an hour after leaving the inn they came to a tree with a large yellow circle painted on it which marked the boundary to the giant's part of the mountain. James told them that even over the storm they would be able to hear the giant's bellow. Sure enough, moments later, they all heard it, and it was just as James said, sadness and oneness with the storm mixed together. The couple and their young son were thoroughly entertained and playfully "frightened."

Lucien walked up close to James so he wouldn't have to speak too loudly and said, "James this is where we part for the evening."

"What do you mean? He's only just begun. He usually goes on for a while longer," James replied.

"Please have our horses and wagons ready to depart. We'll be leaving in the morning and please tell the innkeeper we will settle our bill with him before we leave," Lucien said.

"Wait, you're planning to go up aren't you?" James asked with rising panic in his voice.

"There is nothing to worry about James. We are here to help him, not hurt him," Lucien said.

"But what about yourselves, I see you are well armed but…but he's huge! We've seen the footprints he leaves behind from his trips to get things from the town. What if he kills you all and then takes his anger at violating his border out on the town?" James asked, fear in his voice.

The other three tourists just stared at the two having the conversation. The boy's mouth was gaped in disbelief in what he was hearing; that these strangers were going to confront the giant of Stormville. The entertainment of it all quickly faded.

Lucien placed both his hands on James's shoulders, looked him in the eyes and said, "James I hear your concerns, but I assure you there will be no violence toward anyone. We'll see you in the morning."

Benagar walked up to James and said, "Nothing had better be missing from our wagons or despite what Lucien said there will be violence toward someone."

The companions took their leave of James and the young family, and continued up the mountain.

They could hear that primal roar grow louder as they moved up the mountain. Soon enough the trees opened into a massive clearing. They could all see a huge cave that seemed to have a door affixed to the entrance. There were animal pens off to the side of the cave. The chicken coops were built off of the ground. The chickens were inside the coop to avoid the weather. The enclosure for the pigs was well made. There was a small barn-like structure built at one end of the pen where the pigs could go to get out of the rain and huddle together. They would be appreciative of the fresh cool mud the next morning when the storm passed. The companions could tell the structures and the door to the cave were built with skill. They were built with strength to resist the elements.

In the center of the clearing open to the sky, stood he who they had been searching for, Derian Stein. Just saying he was big was not enough compared to seeing him with one's own eyes. Almost eight feet tall, his back was toward them so the full width of him was evident. He was standing there naked, face towards the sky. It would be easy to assume someone so large would have some fat on him. Not Derian Stein. It was as if he were chiseled from stone. Every inch of him was muscle. Long black hair cascaded down his back, wet from the rain.

In his hand was what seemed to be a long, thick metal pole with an anvil welded to the end of it. He then lifted that makeshift warhammer, about 400 pounds of steel straight up in the air as if it weighed nothing. What the group saw next none of them would ever forget. A bolt of lightning came down and struck the anvil. Lightning coursed down the pole and into Derian. They could see the lightning dancing along the metal discs in his arms and legs. He gave no indication of pain, in fact his bellow turned to one of joy. Just then his head whipped around, and Lucien didn't know if it was a trick of the light, but he could swear he saw the lightning in Derian's eyes.

"Who's there?!" Derian yelled angrily.

Lucien and the group came into the clearing slowly, only holding their lanterns.

"Hello Derian," Lucien said calmly.

"How do you know that name?!" Derian replied still anger in his voice.

"I'm here on behalf of your father," Lucien replied

"You lie!" Derian replied even angrier now.

This was not going the way Lucien had hoped. The air had grown tense with expected violence. Derian was standing there breathing heavy now with his rising anger. All of his considerable muscle tensed. The grip on his hammer/anvil was tightening in his massive fist. It was then that Arissa put her lantern down and began walking slowly towards Derian. Her hands were empty, but her face was full of compassion. She walked until she stood right before what was the largest and obviously mightiest living being anyone had ever seen. If the moment wasn't so serious, it would be comical.

Arissa touched Derian's forearm gently, looked up into his face, smiled and said, "We are here to help you Derian. We are going to take you to your father."

As fast as the anger was in Derian, it was gone. The tension left Derian's body and he dropped his hammer with a heavy thud.

He looked at the group and said, "Please come inside."

The group followed Derian inside and marveled at the home Derian had created from a simple cave. There was a cooking area and even a small forge. There were shelves carved into the walls filled with books. A large pallet of hay covered in animal hide at the back of the cave was where

Derian slept. Derian went and got a robe to put on. His skin had a grey hue to it, something Dr. Stein never mentioned. Lucien couldn't help but wonder how many animals died to make the robe. It was finely made though. Derian put some fresh wood on a fire that was already burning when they entered the cave. There was instantly more light and heat.

"Please excuse me, I don't have visitors so there are no chairs. There is a barrel of fresh rainwater there in the corner with a ladle. Please drink all you want and make yourselves comfortable wherever you would like," Derian said.

The group left their raincloaks and lanterns by the door of the cave. There was plenty of room for all of them in the massive cave and the companions took seats on the floor near the fire. As the group was settling in around the fire, Lucien took the time to really get a look at Derian Stein. He had a heavy brow but overall, his face was a good one. It would not be off the mark to call him handsome. His countenance wasn't fearsome at all. Derian's voice was deep but pleasant to listen to and surprisingly soothing. Lucien then took the time to make introductions.

"Your father told me so much about you Derian I feel like I already know you," Lucien said.

"I feel like you have quite a tale to tell Lucien Farrunner. Please tell it," Derian said.

For the next hour Lucien told Derian his journey, all of it. From how it all began to this very moment. When he was finished there were tears in Derian's eyes. Tears of joy and sadness.

"Lucien I am sorry for all you have lost but glad for all you have gained. To think that you five, all so young, brought about the destruction of the 100 Blades, and you Lucien defeated Kane in single combat, truly amazing," Derian said.

"You know of Kane and the 100 Blades?" Rob asked.

"My father made me very well. Some nights I would come down and listen in on the conversations that would go on at the inn to keep up with the goings on in the world. If I focus I can listen in from a far distance. No one ever knew I was there listening," Derian replied

"Your father was good to me and taught me much. It broke his heart to think of you in the world thinking that he had abandoned you," Lucien said.

"To finally know after all these years what really happened. I don't know what to say or how to thank you. My father said there were good people in this world, but I had lost faith in that long ago." It was then Derian took a deep breath and asked, "So what is next."

"Well, I say we get some rest tonight and tomorrow Derian you gather what you wish to take from here and we begin the journey to rescue your father," Lucien said.

"That is what will happen. You all will stay here with me and tomorrow we begin a new journey. For me, I may not sleep. There is much to ponder," Derian stated matter-of-factly.

The next morning the group awoke shortly after dawn to find Derian already dressed and ready to go. They were all amazed at how he did this without waking any of them. He had a few packs slung around his body, but all in all it didn't seem like he was taking too much with him. His hammer rested on his shoulder as if it weighed nothing. The group gathered their raincloaks and lanterns and began the trek down the mountain. Before they left the clearing for the path downward, Derian stopped and took one last look at the place he called home for almost a century.

"Derian your clothes are well made. The stitching is impeccable," Arissa said.

"Thank you Arissa. My father taught me many practical things, sewing and stitching were two of them," Derian replied.

It wasn't long before the group came upon the inn where a large crowd was waiting for them. To the people of Stormville's credit no fear came over them as they saw Derian with the group, only awe and amazement as they saw a century old legend come to life walking toward them. James was at the forefront of the crowd. The group walked up to him and laid their raincloaks and lanterns at his feet.

"I'll settle up with the inn keep," Quinn said.

"And I'll inspect the wagons," Benagar said as both wagons and horses were waiting just as Lucien asked them to be the night before.

"I, I can't believe it," James said.

"James Lattimore, this is Derian Stein," Lucien introduced.

"It is my pleasure to meet you James Lattimore. Long ago I had many conversations with your ancestor, Rupert Lattimore. He came to me in curiosity and kindness. We spoke of many things, and he never pressed me about who I was or about my past. He preserved my privacy. I mourned his passing. I see his kindness in your face," Derian said to the still stunned James.

"Thank you Derian. That's very kind of you to say," James replied.

"You see James, I told you everything would be alright," Lucien said.

"People of Stormville thank you for respecting my privacy and for the many gifts you have given me over the decades. I wish I had made different choices in the past, perhaps we could have all known each other better. There are animals and other things at my cave that you are all welcome to. I bid you all good fortune and perhaps one day the giant of Stormville will return to see how this special town is doing. Farewell," Derian said. He then made his way through the crowd and began helping Benagar rearrange things between the wagons to better accommodate Derian and his things and to distribute the weight evenly.

"Wait he's leaving with you? What will we do?" James asked.

Lucien pulled James aside so the crowd couldn't hear him, "This town has become very prosperous because of Derian's ideas and presence over the years. Seems to me a clever person could maybe host tours to the place where the giant of Stormville lived. Besides are you going to stop him from leaving?"

"No, of course not," James stuttered at the thought of confronting that massive being.

Lucien could almost see the man's mind working on how to keep the tours going and the money flowing. Derian climbed into a wagon with his hammer and the few things he took from his cave. The wagon creaked a bit, but it held just fine. Quinn climbed into the back with him, and Lucien and Arissa climbed into the driver's seat. The twins were on their horses and Timber and Benagar drove the other wagon. As the teams drove out of town Derian waved goodbye to the people of Stormville and they waved farewell back to him.

"I am excited but also anxious. The last time I ventured out into the world it did not go as well as I would have liked," Derian said.

"Things will be different this time," Lucien said.

"Why?"

"Because this time you are among friends," Lucien replied.

"I've never had a friend,' Derian replied.

"Well now you have many," Arissa said.

Chapter Six

The next few days were full of good-natured conversations and the playful banter of good friends. Derian was asked, and Derian asked, many questions as they all got to know each other.

"Derian your father didn't mention the grey hue to your skin. Has it always been this color?" Lucien asked.

"No, it hasn't. Every time I touched the lightning my skin grew a little darker until it stayed this color. Some sort of side effect I suppose," Derian answered.

"Can I ask why you do it?" Tom asked.

"You all may ask me anything you like, as to the why of it, the best answer I can give is instinct. When I was driven out of Terramilene I was cold and alone, but I felt I was headed in the right direction. As I got closer to Stormville and Stormount, I started to feel drawn there. Lightning had much to do with my creation which is why I believe I was drawn to a place that had frequent storms. One night in my cave, with the storm raging outside, again that feeling of being drawn came over me and I disrobed and walked out into the storm. I lifted my face and arms to the sky and…..nothing happened. I remembered the details of how I came to be, so one night when the town was asleep I snuck down and slipped a piece of paper under the blacksmith's door, asking him if he would create my hammer. A few nights later I came down and checked the area where the people of Stormville left me things and there it was. The next storm I went outside with my hammer, thrust it into the sky and sure enough a bolt of lightning struck it. All of these things I did because I felt drawn to do so. None of it was through intellectual design or from investigating via trial and error," Derian said.

"I have a question I think we've all been wondering," Rob said.

"What is it Rob?" Derian asked.

"What does it feel like when you touch the lightning?"

"You Hollis boys ask fine questions. I'm afraid this one may be as difficult to answer as your brother's, but I will try. It is like I am one with the storm. When the lightning courses through me I feel stronger than is explainable. It is like being a part of one of the primal forces of nature itself. It sometimes intensifies the feelings I've been having, and sometimes it clears my mind. I hope that answers the question for all of you," Derian said.

"It sounds incredible," Arissa said.

"It is."

"I have a theory," Benagar remarked to almost everyone's surprise.

"This ought to be good," Quinn said sarcastically.

"That tab of yours is growing Quinn," Timber said.

Quinn rolled his eyes but remained silent.

"Please, Benagar I would be honored to hear your insights," Derian said.

"Well, it seems to me from all you've said that the storm or the lightning or nature itself was looking out for you when no one else would. You said you were drawn to a place of frequent storms. You then, through memories and instinct, had your hammer built which allowed you to attract the lightning during storms. You were in a place where you were safe. You may have been alone, at least as far as companionship is concerned, but I think that was more your choice than anything else," Benagar said. He deep eyes showing the group how much thought he had given to the response.

There was a stunned look on everyone's except for Timber's face. The big warrior spoke with everyone of course, but usually the sentences were short with a lot of grunts involved. This was the longest anyone, but Timber had heard him speak. In this moment Lucien realized why his uncle insisted these two go with him. What Benagar said made complete sense and showed that the big wolf had depth of thought and wisdom. It was a wonder why he hid it.

"Thank you Benagar. I have never thought of it that way, but your theory is sound. This gives me a new perspective on my time being secluded. To think that something was watching over me gives me great comfort," Derian said.

"Do you still feel drawn to Stormount?" Benagar asked.

Derian took a moment, looked back the way they had come, and closed his eyes. When he re-opened them he said, "No, I don't. Not at all. Interesting."

"My belief on that is because whatever was looking out for you now knows that you are, and will be, surrounded by people looking out for you," Benagar said. With that Benagar gave a snap on the reins and pulled ahead of Lucien's wagon.

Lucien and Arissa looked at one another, confounded by what had transpired over the few minutes the two wagons rode next to each other and what Benagar's piece in all of it was.

The remaining portion of the day there was lighthearted conversation and Derian began to recall what it meant to joke and have talks with people who wanted or needed nothing from him other than him being present.

Late that evening Lucien asked Timber to join him in the task of washing dishes in a nearby stream. When they reached the stream and began cleaning dishes Timber said, "So Lucien, what do you want to ask me?"

"Timber what makes a good leader?" Lucien asked.

"A good question Lucien, but unfortunately there is no simple answer. There are many variables. The type of person the leader is, the type of men being led, the types of situations, and the way the leader handles such situations. As horrible a person as Kane was, an argument could be made that he was a good leader, if not a moral leader. For ten years he kept his men free and paid. They feared him personally but respected him as their leader. Lucien do you want to know if you are a good leader?" Timber asked.

"Am I?"

"Yes, Lucien, and here are the reasons why as far as Benagar and I see them. It's much more than the fact that for your first mission you had a good plan, or that this mission you have knowledge of where we are going. You formed your bonds at the Citadel with your friends, and when you all graduated, they followed you into danger because they love you and *want* to follow you. Part of it is your story. It's inspiring Lucien. You've lost and endured so much, but you keep moving forward. You have inner strength that others see. Your cousin Quinn saw that strength and was filled with familial pride. The prince feels deeply for you. He first saw you as long-lost family, as someone who treated him with respect because of who he was as a man, not as royalty. That has now turned to pride in you and he has become part of your group, has he not?" Timber asked.

"He has," Lucien said with a smile.

"The truest definition of heroism has now been added to all of you. You all did what almost all thought impossible. You defeated Kane individually and then you all destroyed the 100 Blades as a group. Soon, your names and the legacy of that situation will be known throughout all of Arborreah. Now this mission. You are keeping your word to a friend and putting yourself in danger to do it. Your friends follow you into that danger, again, willingly, and easily because they love you. I believe the future is in good hands with young heroes such as yourselves. I believe you have added another member to your group in Derian. You feel that don't you?" Timber asked.

"I do," Lucien said.

"He is remarkable in so many ways. To be who, and what, he is and to have endured all that time in his own thoughts of loneliness but still have a calm mind and demeanor is a testament to him. I know he will make a fine addition to your group," Timber said.

"What about you two?" Lucien asked.

"Ah young Lucien, Benagar and I are enjoying our time with you all, but there is a gap that is more than generational. You understand what that means. You and your friends time in life is just beginning, while our time, while not over, is waning. Benagar and I are very fond of you all and would follow you Lucien wherever you lead for the time, but it will not last long. When this mission is done I expect our time with you will be as well. I hope I answered your question Lucien," Timber said as he turned and took his share of the dishes back to camp.

Lucien smiled, grabbed his clean dishes, and followed after Timber. He was both grateful and happy to have had the conversation with the wise counsel, but also felt a twinge of sadness at the thought of the two guardsmen not being on whatever adventures lay ahead.

Before the companions turned northeast for the mountain paths that would lead to the great desert and the land of Kabaal, they came to the town of Algernon. Aside from the great kingdoms, cities, and farming communities, a majority of Arborreah was made up of small towns. Some that just provided a place to eat or sleep before going back on the road to someplace better. Algernon was not one of those towns. It had become a fairly large town over the years, and it all started because of fish.

When the settlers of Algernon started their town they didn't realize what they had stumbled upon. They built their town near a portion of the Scoggin river where the great salmon staged before their spawning migration upriver through the mountain streams. Those streams were hidden in deep-set gorges where no one could get to. If the great salmon wasn't caught in Algernon, they were never going to be caught.

The fish, more so than anywhere else, were especially tasty due to the rare minerals found in the Scoggin river, and when word got out about the delicacy of those fish people travelled from far and wide to taste them.

It wasn't long before the leaders of Algernon realized they had something that would bring value to their town. They found they could charge high prices for the fish and people would be more than happy to pay. Adding to the desire to buy fish, many of those visitors needed places to sleep and eat while in Algernon. The town quickly grew.

Eventually the townspeople made a deal with the Citadel of the Mages, which allowed students in training to stay in Algernon and practice cold magic. The mage would make huge quantities of ice. The fish was either put on ice, or salt, and would then be sent by wagon to many places all over the land. People who would never be able to travel to Algernon were grateful to have shipments arrive unspoiled. The town found the perfect balance of caring for the great fish by not depleting the spawning grounds, and still creating a revenue for their community. They kept the natural cycle going and Algernon prospered.

The companions passed under the finely made gate and into Algernon in the mid-afternoon. There were guards at the gate, but they just looked the group over and waved them on. The town was larger and cleaner than Stormville. The people were friendly enough. Some waved, some didn't. There was some eyes that went wide when they saw Derian, but no outright fear. As is found in most towns, many inns and businesses lined the streets. They finally found an inn with a large enough stable for their wagons. It was called the Fisherman's Rest, a large inn near the docks and warehouses by the river. Benagar kept the same theme as Stormville and terrorized the stableboys while the rest of the group went inside.

Derian had to duck to enter the inn. The patrons and the barkeep looked up to see who entered, and again some were surprised at Derian's size, but none showed fear. The group made their way to the bar where the barkeep greeted them.

"Welcome to the Fisherman's Rest travelers. Jack Anders, owner, what can I do for you folks?" he asked.

"Thank you Jack. Well first we have twelve horses and two large wagons being taken care of in your stables now. I have what may be a strange request. I doubt you have a bed that can accommodate my friend Derian here. My proposal is this: we will pay the price of four rooms if you would just make sure fresh hay is put down in the stables. We would not sleep in soft beds while our friend slept in the stables by himself," Lucien said.

"Lucien that is not necessary. There is no reason you all shouldn't get a good night's rest. I'll be fine in the stable,' Derian said.

"We stick together my friend," Lucien replied.

"Gentleman please, how does this sound? Rent the four rooms. Each room has two large beds. Place one of the mattresses on the floor. I will have some of the boys move an extra mattress into the room and place it on the floor next to the other mattress. The combined mattresses should be more than big enough to attend to this young man's needs," Jack said.

"Even better. Thank you Jack," Lucien replied.

"Wonderful! Now I would be a poor inkeep indeed if I didn't recognize hungry, thirsty, and weary travelers. Please retire to the dining area. Feel free to move the chairs and tables around to meet your needs. There is a sturdy couch, that if you don't sit in the middle will support you Derian. I'll have cold ales brought to you all," Jack said.

"Thank you Jack, you've been very kind," Lucien said.

"Do you have any mead?" Arissa asked.

"I'm afraid I don't miss. I apologize. We do have a cider that has fermented. Have a taste and if you like it we can bring that to your table with the ales," Jack replied.

Arissa took the sip and didn't hide the scrunch of her forehead.

"I'll take that as a no," Jack laughed.

"Ale for me please. Thank you," Arissa said.

"My pleasure. Now will you pay as you go, or would you like to run a tab?" Jack asked.

"We'll run a tab," Quinn said.

"Excellent young sir, there is just one more thing, you must check your weapons here with me. It is a town ordinance not mine. I will keep them in a locked room behind the bar where they will be safe until you leave. By the looks of you I doubt anyone with weapons would put up much of a fight against you without your weapons," Jack attempted to joke. He was a little disappointed not to get a laugh from anyone in the group.

The group complied with the ordinance and turned over their considerable number of weapons to Jack for safekeeping. The companions adjourned to the dining area where they moved some tables and chairs around so they could all sit together. The couch held Derian and a few moments later two lovely young waitresses arrived with their ales. They were refreshingly cold.

Quinn and the twins immediately began flirting with the waitresses. The two girls received the attention good naturedly, but their interest was mostly in Derian. They openly flirted with him touching his arms and hair. What was more fascinating to everyone was Derian himself. He had the two girls giggling with clever jokes he told in his deep voice. He did not act like someone who had very little contact with people, let alone pretty girls, in the last hundred years. When the girls left, everyone was staring at Derian.

"How did you do that?" Tom asked.

"Do what?" Derian replied.

"You had those two girls eating out of your hand," Rob said.

Derian just smiled and said, "Like I said my father taught me many things."

"Ha! Ha! Ha! Oh Derian, I knew you would fit right in," Quinn said.

They had another fabulous meal together of thick salmon steaks, potatoes, and greens. They also switched from ale to bottles of red and white wine which both went better with the salmon. The Fisherman's Rest began to fill with customers as the workday ended. Some went straight to the bar some sat down for a meal. As people came in they looked the group over, took notice of Derian, again without real fear, and some nodded in greeting. Some men began to re-arrange the center of the room. They put a large circular table in the center of the room and put chairs around it. They were large men, heavily muscled, and the smell of salmon came off of them. Probably warehouse workers whose strength would be needed moving around boxes weighing hundreds of pounds of salmon each day.

"Excuse me miss," Timber said to a passing waitress.

"Yes sir,"

"What are those men doing?" he asked.

"Those be the boys from the warehouse. They are getting ready to play Kings. It's payday. They play every payday," she replied.

"Is it a private game or can anyone play?" Timber asked.

"No sir not private. I'm sure if you ask for a seat they won't mind," she said.

"Thank you miss," Timber said while giving her a silver piece.

"You're welcome sir," she replied.

"You think that's a good idea Timber?" Benagar asked.

"I think it's a great idea mother. You know how hard it is for me to get a proper game anymore. Everything will be fine, you'll see," Timber replied as he put his hand on Benagar's shoulder as he got up to go ask for a seat at the game.

"Gentlemen, my name is Timber Greenleaf, a traveler through your fine town. I was told you were about to play Kings and would ask if you would allow me to join," Timber asked

"Sure stranger, pull up a chair. Your money is as good as any. I'm Jerry, this is Marty, Harlan, Wally, and Earnest."

"Thank you gents, allow me to buy the first round," Timber said as he sat down and rolled up his sleeves.

Lucien saw a burrow of the big wolf's brow and asked, "Benagar what's wrong?"

"Does Timber lose all of his money?" Arissa asked.

Benagar took in a deep breath, let it out, and began, "Remember when Timber told you all about our wild days, getting into fights at many inns and taverns at many towns?"

The group besides Derian nodded.

"Quite a few times the reason for those fights were because of Timber. Arissa, you asked me if Timber loses all his money. Quite the contrary. He never loses. He never backs down. He won't lose a small hand to appease the other players. He feels they should be better at the game. Before you know it he's being accused of cheating and the fists start flying," Benagar said.

"So, what do we do," asked Quinn.

"We all have Timber's back. Spread out into different parts of the room. The fact that no weapons are allowed means it shouldn't get too bad. There are no bouncers which tells me this bar doesn't get a lot of trouble. Just watch each other's backs, there are more locals than there are of us. Don't hurt anyone more than you must," Benagar said as he got up from the table. He turned back one more time, this time with a big smile, "And oh yeah have some fun."

Lucien, Arissa, and Derian stood at the bar. Rob and Tom were diagonally across the room from them, flirting and nursing ales. Lucien could tell though that they were watching carefully. Quinn was in another corner of the room doing the same as the twins. Benagar sort of hovered around in the general area behind Timber.

"Do you know this game Lucien," asked Derian.

"My father and many of the men in my village played sometimes. My father tried to explain it to me one time when I was young, but I had no head for the many rules at that time and lost interest in it. I never got the sense though that they were as passionate about the game as Benagar says Timber is," Lucien replied.

"I think maybe we should have Timber teach us while on the road," Derian said.

"I think that's a fine idea," Derian replied.

It all started out just fine. Everyone around the game table was laughing, drinking, and having a good time. With each hand that Timber won the mood slowly changed. The laughing and smiling gradually ended, and the rising smell of anger and frustration came off the men playing. Lucien met eyes with Quinn. Quinn had stopped flirting and now was just watching, the same with thc twins. They didn't need a werewolf's sense of smell to know that things at the table had changed. Benagar stopped moving about and now stood behind Timber.

"Kings!" Timber shouted as he laid down his cards for another win.

"Impossible! No one can be that lucky!," Harlan the largest man at the table shouted as he stood up so fast his chair went flying out from behind him.

"Take it easy, Harlan," Jack said from behind the bar.

"Stay out of this Jack, this is between us and the cheat, it's got nothing to do with you," Harlan replied.

"You're about to start trouble at my inn so I'd say it concerns me. His sleeves have been rolled up the entire time you boys have been playing. How exactly did he cheat?" Jack asked.

"I don't know how he's doing it, but like I said nobody's that lucky," Harlan replied angrily.

"I assure you sir luck has nothing to do with it, just all of your bad card play," Timber said.

Lucien dropped and shook his head at the same time, knowing that comment from Timber did not help things.

The man named Harlan moved to stand directly in front of Timber. He looked down at the much smaller man and said through gritted teeth, "Cheat."

Benagar then stepped in front of Timber to stand face to face with Harlan, the two big men were practically the same size.

"If you call my friend a cheat again you better count your teeth first," Benagar said.

"DON'T YOU DO IT HARLAN," Jack warned. Even the owner of the inn knew there were lines that couldn't be crossed, and Harlan must have had a history of crossing a lot of lines.

Harlan gave Benagar a smirk, looked around him, made eye contact with Timber and said, "Cheat."

He then punched Benagar in the face with a short but powerful right hook.

Benagar barely moved. He rubbed his jaw, smiled, then shot a straight jab into Harlan's face breaking his nose. Then chaos broke out.

Jerry grabbed Timber and Marty started punching Benagar's best friend in the side of the face.

Faster than any in the dining area could comprehend, Quinn leapt over a table and crashed into Wally and Earnest, who were looking to join in the punching of a bound-up Timber. All three crashed to the floor in a heap of flailing limbs.

The twins intercepted other locals who went to help their friends against these strangers. Even without their staves the boys were untouchable against men who had no training in fighting. Local after local stepped in an attempt to break the wall of the twins only to find themselves looking up at the twins from the floor wondering how they got there.

Lucien and Arissa made quick work of the two working over Timber.

Jack yelled from the bar for everyone to stop but no one listened.

A young man tried to sneak up on Derian to smash a chair over his broad back. In all the noise of screaming, cussing and items being broken, Derian knew the young man was behind him. There were no sudden movements, Derian turned his head, looked the young man in the eyes, and frowned. The young boy audibly gulped, put the chair down and walked quickly out the door.

The locals quickly surmised that while they had the numbers they definitely did not have the skills, or the desire. One by one they backed down or raised their hands, indicating they were finished. Eventually everyone was done except for Harlan and Benagar who continued trading punches. To the fisherman's credit he had some boxing skill and Benagar's face had the lumps to prove it. But Benagar was still smiling, and Harlan was breathing heavy. The big local was feeling good about his chances until he threw a quick left jab and Benagar deftly caught it in his palm and then threw a lighting fast uppercut that put Harlan on his ass. Benagar moved toward the downed man, but Harlan put his hand up.

"I yield. Damn you hit hard," Harlan said, spitting out blood and a tooth.

"You too. Who taught you how to fight?" Benagar asked as he held out his hand to Harlan to help him up.

"My father, and you?" Harlan asked looking up at the first person to put him on his butt.

"My father," Benagar replied, still offering his hand

"How about we have an ale and drink to our fathers," Harlan asked, as he wiped his palms of dust from the floor and then took the meaty paw that had just busted his tooth out.

"Apologize to my friend first," Benagar said as his opponent stood.

"You're right. Timber I apologize for calling you a cheat. You and your friends are visitors to our town, and it should have been a trouble free visit. I've never seen anyone play like you. I could blame the ale or the fact I was watching my pay disappear to a stranger but there is no excuse. Will you accept my apology?" Harlan asked.

"Of course, Harlan," Timber replied as they shook hands. Timber had a split lip and an eye that was swelling by the second. Both would be gone in a few hours.

"I wish to give you and your friends your money back," Timber began.

"No, you won it fair and square," Harlan said.

"Please I insist. My friends and I came here to enjoy a fine meal and sleep in a warm bed before continuing our journey. I hadn't played Kings in a while. I became overzealous and played too hard. The last thing I came here to do was take the wages of hard-working men such as yourselves," Timber said.

"Thank you Timber, we will accept your gracious generosity as long as you allow us to buy the next round," Harlan replied.

"Deal," Timber said.

And just like that the men who punched each other in the face moments before were now drinking and smiling again as if nothing happened. Lucien found himself a little dumbfounded.

"Jack I'm sorry about all this. When we leave tomorrow morning please add any damages to our tab," Lucien said to the bartender.

"Thank you, you are very gracious young man. I can see your friend, Quinn I believe, handing out silver pieces to my waitresses and the young men who work for me. Very generous indeed," Jack said.

"Well, it's only right, after all they are cleaning up the mess we made," Lucien replied.

The rest of the night was spent much as it began with laughing and drinking. This time there was some nursing of cuts and bruises. Benagar put Harlan's nose back in place for him. Eventually though the locals left for home with hands being shook all around and the companions turned in for the evening. Lucien and Arissa went to their room which was clean and cozy.

"I see that thoughtful look on your face," Arissa teased.

"Ha! Just pondering this evening's events. I'm not troubled just a bit confused," Lucien replied.

"Well, I won't have it. Stop your pondering right now and save it for tomorrow. While the ale doesn't invoke the same type of craziness as the mead, I'm still feeling very good. We have privacy tonight and many un-private nights ahead of us, so I will have all of you tonight," Arissa said.

"I think I can manage that m'lady," Lucien replied smiling.

Chapter Seven

The next morning the group woke up early and came downstairs to find Jack and his staff already up and preparing for the day. The group decided to have a breakfast of oatmeal and fruit while Jack's stableboys prepared their horses and wagons for travel. When they were finished Quinn went to take care of their bill. He felt Jack had actually under charged them, and for the next three minutes Quinn and Jack haggled on the final bill. They eventually fell in the middle and shook hands. One by one they collected their weapons from Jack, except for Derian and Quinn who never came in with any, and thanking him for his hospitality. Lucien was last.

"Thank you Jack and again I apologize for all the trouble last night," Lucien said.

"And again, young man, nothing to worry about. Harlan lost his temper, not the first time, and you and your friends were nothing but fine polite guests. Safe travels," Jack said.

"Thank you 'til we meet again," Lucien said and walked out the door.

Everyone was waiting for him as he climbed into the driver's seat of a wagon. Arissa was next to him on the seat with Derian in the back. Timber, Benagar, and Quinn were in the other wagon, while twins rode their horses. As they were leaving town they saw the men from last night coming toward them, heading toward the pier and a long day's work.

"Safe travels my friends," Harlan said with a smile that had a gap in his teeth, two black eyes from his broken nose, and an oversized bottom lip.

"May you have a fine catch today and every day," Benagar replied.

The companions left Algernon and turned northeast for the mountain roads, and then Kabaal. The road was wide, and the wagons rode side by side with Rob next to Lucien's wagon and Tom next to Quinn's.

"So, Lucien are you going to ask your question or make us wait all day for it?" Timber asked.

"You two wanted that fight last night didn't you?" Lucien asked.

"I don't know if *wanted* is the right word," Timber replied.

"Then what word would you use?" Lucien asked.

"Needed?" Timber replied.

"Why?"

"Ah Lucien, I do enjoy your questions, they never have easy answers. I suppose the simple answer would be…..life," Timber said.

"How do you mean?" Lucien asked

"Well Lucien, every man and woman, no matter what their station in life, be it king or pauper, faces pressure, worries, anxiety, and whatever life puts in their path. Everyone handles this pressure in different ways. Some handle it in better ways than others, some in worse ways. Only the very young and very old don't feel life's pressure. The very young have no real responsibilities yet, and the very old are just trying to enjoy what is left of their life before they pass on."

"Gar and I love King Killian. We ran together and got into trouble and adventure when we were young, but when he decided to settle down and become a responsible king, husband, and father, we also left behind our wild ways to become his personal guard. We don't regret our decision. Frankly we didn't trust anyone else to do the job properly. Killian tried to dissuade us, but we wouldn't hear it. He tried to keep us busy and active. Being the king's personal guard doesn't just mean hovering over him every hour of every day. We are his right hand and sometimes his fist. That's actually why Gar and I weren't there when you all first arrived at the Great Wood. We were away taking care of a matter for the king."

"Arborreah has been at peace for a long time, and we would have it no other way but, and this is the important part I would have you all hear; we are the warriors. Wolves of action. People who have trained and trained hard. We take pride in our skills and strive to make those skills better. But what do you do when there is no foe to fight or battle to win? Training and sparring can help but it's not the same. The Citadel trains you to control your emotions to concentrate and focus them so they don't overwhelm you, but you can't meditate all day long. I see the value of it, truly. I see young Derian take part in your morning meditations," Timber said.

"Everyone is welcome to join us," Arissa said.

"Yes and we are grateful for the invitation, Arissa but I think Gar and I are pretty set in our ways. As far as Prince Quinn goes he is too young to be so stubborn," Timber said.

"I'm not being stubborn. I see everyone's skills and yes they are impressive, it's just that when it comes to battle my instincts right now tell me fighting with claw and fang is the way I am most comfortable," Quinn replied.

"Would it kill you to pick up a sword at least?" Benagar said.

"Don't worry old bull when that time comes I'll be sure to let you know," Quinn replied as he quickly moved to the back of the wagon out of smacking range from Benagar who did not like to be called old.

"Young Hollis's, you come from a large and prosperous farming community. You both seemed at ease with last night's action. My instincts tell me you may have seen or heard something similar, am I right?" Timber asked.

"You are," the twins answered in unison.

"You all know we come from a vast farming community and everyone for the most part is happy. If one farmer happens to have a bad crop, we all pull together and help him. No one goes hungry or cold. But the work is hard. Up at dawn in at dusk. My father says farming is a calling and he's right. We would see him sometimes looking out at our fields with such pride. There were times he would come in from the day's work exhausted with nary a complaint. Sometimes the men would gather at the inn in town for a few hours and drink and play Kings. Sometimes someone would drink too much, call someone a cheat, and a fight would break out. No one would truly be hurt, and when it was over, all would be forgiven.

We saw this happen one time when our father convinced our mother to let us go to town with him and watch the game. We were behind the bar when we saw the game go from friends playing a game, to friends fighting. On the way home we asked why he and his friends were fighting. He told us not to worry, that they were still friends, and sometimes men just had to be men. We didn't really understand then but after listening to you Timber I think we do," Rob said

"Boy our mother gave our father a tongue lashing the next morning when she saw the bruise on his face," Tom said smiling at the memory.

"I think last night reminded us of that night. We felt the thing you were talking about Timber. Just men, or women, releasing the pressure of their lives. I think you can be happy with your life, but still need a release every now and again," Rob finished.

"Very well said young Hollis'. If you think about it Lucien you already know about this release of pressure," Timber said.

"I do?" Lucien said.

"Your fight with Kane. You told us yourself that before the fight started you had to focus. To take all you were feeling, all that pain, rage, and fear, and compress it into a tiny flame or those feelings left uncontrolled would have been the death of you. So, what happened? You delivered the killing blow, whispered in Kane's ear who you are, then tore his throat out with your fangs, ripped his head off and put it on a pike. If that's not a release of pressure I don't know what is. You think that example too intense. All right is there no fight you fought, that did not result in death, that you took pleasure in?" Timber asked.

Arissa entered the conversation, answering for Lucien, by saying, "Berros."

"I was defending your honor," Lucien said.

"You were Lucien, but we were there and there was an aspect of joy on your face as you fought and beat him," Tom said.

"You are right. If I am being honest, yes making him apologize to Arissa was paramount, but I enjoyed defeating someone who half our class thought was my equal in hand-to-hand combat," Lucien replied.

"Was this boy hurt badly?" Timber asked.

"Not any more than I had to," Lucien replied.

"Before the fight started did you want to kill this boy?" Timber asked.

"No," Lucien said.

"Think upon last night Lucien, before the fight began, what did you smell, what did your instincts tell you?" Timber asked.

"There was anger, frustration, and violence in the air," Lucien replied.

"Murderous violence?" Timber asked.

"No…..,"

"Truth is Lucien, Gar and I have been in many bars, inns, and taverns where the feel of murderous bloodshed was thick. I would never have played Kings in a place like that. I love the game, but no one should die because of a game of cards. So last night's bit of action was merely that, a bit of action. We knew everyone would be fine including all of you. Does this make sense?" Timber asked..

"It does Timber. Thank you," Lucien said once again reminding himself how thankful he was his uncle sent these two remarkable wolves with him and his friends. His uncle wanted him to take advantage of their wisdom and he was going to.

"Oh, don't worry Timber. Lucien and Arissa know all about releasing built up pressure," Quinn said with a wicked smirk.

"I think you'll be paying dearly for that comment," Derian said.

"Most assuredly he will" Lucien said as Arissa glared at Quinn.

"Just leave a little for me Arissa. I still owe him for two *old* comments," Benagar said

"No promises," Arissa answered without taking her glare off of Quinn.

Quinn could only smile as he looked forward and sped his horses up a little, taking the lead position of the wagons.

Two uneventful days through the mountain roads and the group reached the border of the great desert that led to the kingdom of Kabaal. That night the group went over the plan of the mission, like they had done many times on their journey. There were no complaints as everyone knew how vital it was for each individual to know their part to perfection.

Derian and Arissa would stay behind. Derian was too heavy for any wolf to carry, even one as large as Gar. From the beginning, Arissa had stated that Derian should not be left alone. If she was needed, she was ready, but the plan had her staying behind. If there was a chance encounter with a band of slave traders they would wish they came upon anyone else beside the duo of Derian and Arissa. Indeed, it would take more than anything the forest could produce for the two staying behind to be in danger of anything, or anyone.

"I cannot thank you all enough for what you are about to do. I wish to see my father again, and I wish to see all of you with him. Be careful, all of you," Derian said. He then hugged each member of the group. Even the hardened Benagar accepted a hug from the giant.

The three-day trip through the desert was filled with nothing but heat and Quinn complaining about the heat, every chance he could. Thay arrived at the gates of Oasis just as the sun was arising on the third day. Lucien, Quinn, Timber, and Benagar, were posing as linen merchants, something Oasis always traded in. The twins posed as armed escorts.

Uninterested human guards, still trying to wake up, saw the linens in the back of the wagon and waved them through. Human guards were used at the gates and not the undead puppets of Igorrian Al-Saam, who were not suited for the task. Lucien, and the team, arrived early enough to find a place in the market area to set up their fake business. Once the tent was set up the six men went inside and closed the flaps giving them the privacy they needed to unload the rest of what they needed for the plan which was hidden underneath the linens.

"Well, so far so good," Rob said.

"Alright in a few hours the merchant area will be up and running for business. Rob and Tom you'll be handling the selling of the linen. Remember people here love to haggle," Lucien said.

"These people have never seen the Hollis boys haggle. Hope you can carry us and all the gold we'll make," Tom said.

"Which will go right back to Rory," Lucien said.

"Oh alright," Rob said.

"Benagar and Quinn will stay here with the boys and guard the tent, wagon, and horses while the boys sell. Timber and I will take a walk to the part of the city where the rich live and see if anything has changed as far as the guards go at

Dr. Stein's house. After returning we wait until nightfall, then execute the next part of the plan. Understood? Any questions?" Lucien inquired.

"Agreed," everyone replied and then went about their individual tasks.

Chapter Eight

After the day's business linens in the marketplace closed, the group gathered in the tent to put the next part of their plan in motion. Quinn, Timber, and Benagar, began wrapping Lucien and Tom from head to toe in linen strips. Then the pieces of armor and weapons were added. Rory's quartermaster supplied what Lucien described to him exactly. Some pieces were altered from existing armor and some custom made. The disguises weren't perfect, but the ruse should hold up under scrutiny, especially at night.

Lucien and Tom would go ahead first. Tom and Lucien had watched Oasis' undead soldiers all day and had their movements and the way they walked down perfectly. Benagar, Timber, and Quinn would follow next with the horses and wagon and wait just before the bend in the road leading to Master Stein's house. Their enhanced senses would serve to know if any trouble was coming their way, while still being close enough to provide aid if anything went wrong. Rob had to stay behind and watch the tent. It would be suspicious if anyone noticed an unattended merchant's tent, and the boys made quite a bit of money from the day's business that had to be guarded.

Lucien and Tom stepped out of the back of the tent, saw no one was around, and began their slow measured walk down the road leading to the wealthy part of the city. They learned breathing techniques from the Citadel so if anyone looked it would look like they weren't breathing at all. They walked in perfect step and neither made a sound as they walked through the front gates and toward the front doors where the first guards awaited. They walked with their backs perfectly straight and eyes forward. They passed the guards, opened the doors, and went inside. They shut the doors and then turned towards the doorway leading down to the lab. There were two guards framing the doorway, letting Lucien and Tom know the master was indeed in his lab. They walked up to the guards and with perfect timing, both Lucien and Tom thrust their spears through the wrapped faces of the two guards, and into their brains, destroying both instantly. Tom waited at the top of the stairs, while Lucien ran down the steps. Lucien pulled down enough wrappings to uncover his mouth and said quietly. "Dr. Stein."

"Lucien? Lucien! You returned!" Master Stein exclaimed.

"Of course I did."

"My boy?" Master Stein asked, tears welling in his eyes.

"Waiting for us in the mountains at the edge of the dessert with my friend Arissa" Lucien replied.

"Is he alright. Did he…" Master Stein started.

"Master Stein there will be plenty of time for questions, right now I need you to listen and do exactly as I say," Lucien said.

After Lucien told Master Stein the plan, they emptied a chest and carried it upstairs. Lucien introduced Tom, and then put the wrappings back over his mouth. He and Tom then threw the guards down the steps. They then carried the chest to the closed front doors and set it down.

"You two take this chest out into the desert and bury it. There are dangerous chemicals in it so don't drop it. I'm retiring for the evening," Master Stein said loud enough for the guards outside the doors to hear.

This practice was done on a regular enough basis to not raise suspicion. Chemicals would get old and while no longer useful they were still too dangerous to just leave lying around. Thankfully there were miles of desert around the city where they could be disposed of safely. Dr. Stein then got inside the chest. Lucien and Tom then picked up the chest, opened the doors, and walked outside. They set the chest down, closed the doors, and began to walk down the path leading away from Master Stein's home.

The guards at the door never moved. The boys kept a steady pace as the chest and the master inside were not that heavy. They rounded the bend which put them out of sight from the master's home to find the wagon waiting for them. Benagar and Timber were in the back of the wagon, and they helped the boys get the chest into the back of it. They helped the doctor out of the chest and gave the doctor a hooded cloak to wear. They were taking no chances of anyone recognizing him. Lucien and Tom began walking back to the marketplace and their tent. While their adrenaline pumped hard through their veins, they did well to maintain the pace and cadence of any of the other guards. Keeping any possible eyes uninterested in their movements.

Quinn would wait ten minutes before starting the wagon back to the tent. A wagon being led by two of the city's guards may draw notice.

Quinn snapped the reigns to begin the short journey back to the marketplace when almost immediately a man literally came out of the shadows from the side of the road. He was dressed all in black and armed. He held up his hand and said, "Hold! It's very late for a ride."

Another Shadowman, for that's who they were, Kabaal's elite warriors, emerged from the shadows behind the wagon, and took up a position there.

"Hello! My uncles and I came here with my grandfather to sell linens in your beautiful city. We thought we would take my grandfather for a ride to see your city in the evening when it was cooler and not as crowded. We were just headed back to our tent in the merchant's quarter." Quinn explained.

"What is in that chest?" asked the Shadowman at the back of the wagon.

"Actually nothing good sir," Timber answered.

"I will see for myself," he replied as he jumped into the wagon with athletic grace.

It's unclear what the Shadowman in the wagon noticed, but he made a gesture to his partner at the front of the wagon.

The Shadowman in the wagon went for his sword, but Timber deftly grabbed the elite warrior's arm so he couldn't draw his blade. Benagar slipped behind the guard and wrenched his head violently to the right. Everyone heard his neck snap. The Shadowman in the front of the wagon brought a whistle to his mouth. If he blew it, all would be lost. A spear erupted through the front of his throat, ending the threat. Lucien and Tom hurried to the wagon.

"Sorry we didn't get here sooner. Lucien heard what was happening, and we moved as fast as we could without drawing attention. From the looks of it we got here just in time," Tom said.

"We have to hide these bodies fast," Lucien said.

"Well, we do have this large chest," Benagar said.

After a few snapped bones later, they stuffed the bodies in the chest, while Lucien and Tom covered the blood in the road with dirt. The interruption had caused a delay in timing. They were so close to completing this mission they could not afford to alter anything going forward. Unwanted attention could still ruin everything.

With as much haste as they could afford the wagon made it back to the tent.

"I was getting worried," Rob said.

"Went off without a hitch," Tom said. His brother knew instantly the response was a lie.

The boys got out of their wrappings and armor and re-dressed as the others gathered what they would need for the run across the desert. They piled in the wagon and rode out the front gates down the main road leading away from the city. When they were far enough away so they wouldn't be seen from the city, they stopped the wagon and got out. They gathered the gold they made from the linen sales, food, waterskins, then walked far away from the horses so as not to terrify them when Quinn, Timber, and Benagar transformed into third form. Rob and Tom were sad they had to leave the horses behind, but there was no other choice. Speed and endurance were needed now. The three transformed and Lucien instructed Master Stein on where to hold, and how to ride.

"I've never seen a werewolf transform before. I have so many questions," Dr. Stein said.

"You'll have time for them all, but for now freedom and your son awaits," Lucien said with a smile.

Lucien and the doctor climbed on Benagar, Rob went with Timber and Tom went with Quinn. Then, in a silent flash of speed, the three werewolves, and their riders, were rushing over the cool night and cooler sand.

Chapter Nine

"It's a beautiful sunrise, isn't it Derian?" Arissa asked as she stretched out her arms high above her head

"Yes it is Arissa," Derian replied. His frame putting Arissa into a shadow.

"Don't hog the warmth of the sun!" Arissa stated. She pushed his hip with all her strength, and he didn't even budge.

Derian smiled at the attempt and kept his arms stretched out over the front of wherever Arissa tried moving to, keeping the sun all to himself.

Over the few days of waiting and worrying about their friends, Arissa and Derian's friendship grew. Each found the other very easy to talk with. She shared with him about her life before the Citadel and how difficult it was, and that being why she has had such a difficult time trusting people.

Derian shared about his years of loneliness and how he believed he would never have someone to talk to for the rest of his life. He mentioned how similar their lives were in the sense of finding friends who they could believe were there to do the best they could for them, instead of lying and using them.

Arissa agreed and opened up about her feelings for Lucien and he promised to keep her words between them. They laughed together, they shed tears together, they laughed about shedding tears. She was amazed at how much care and gentleness filled Derian's large size. He was amazed at how much strength filled her small size.

"Don't worry Derian. I know Lucien. If something was wrong, I would feel it. I would. Everything is going to be fine. They will all be back soon, and you and your father will be reunited," Arissa said.

"I think that's what I am nervous about," Derian said.

"What do you mean?"

"It has been a century since we've seen each other. What if he's disappointed in me? What if his feelings have changed for some reason?" Derian said.

"Do you trust Lucien, Derian?" Arissa asked.

"I do."

"Then trust the things he told you that your father confided in him. That you awakened parts of his heart that he thought was dead forever. The parts that love and care for others. That his heart broke every day he thought that you might think he abandoned you. Everything is going to be alright Derian," Arissa said.

"Thank you Arissa. It seems we are about to find out soon. They are coming," Derian said.

"Really? I don't see anything," Arissa said.

"My father made me very well. I can see very far and also in the dark. A few more minutes and you will see," Derian said.

A few minutes later she could see them and after counting to make sure they were all accounted for Arissa let out a sigh of relief. She watched as the group stopped where the desert met the mountains. She watched as the riders dismounted and the wolves transformed back to their human form. She watched them put on robes the riders had for them and make their way toward her and Derian's camp. One by one they came up the trail to be greeted with hugs by Arissa. Then came the man who could only be Dr. Stein.

"Master Stein my name is Arissa. I've been waiting here with your son," Arissa said.

"Very nice to meet you Arissa. Lucien says my son could not be in better company," Master Stein replied.

"Hello father," Derian said quietly with his head down. The wolves could smell fear, anxiousness, and sadness from the giant.

"My son," Dr. Stein replied almost as quietly.

He then walked over to his son, looked up into his face and said, "Come down here son, I'm afraid I haven't discovered how to make myself taller yet."

Derian knelt down and Dr. Stein embraced his son's massive neck and Derian embraced his father. All the group could hear for the next few minutes was quiet crying and Dr. Stein saying over and over. "My son. I am so sorry. I am so very sorry. How I've missed you..."

"Gar are you crying?" Timber asked.

"Of course not. We just ran through the desert. There is sand in my eye," Benagar replied.

"That does make sense since you trailed behind us the whole way," Quinn said.

"I carried two!" Benagar exclaimed.

Quinn left it at that with a nudge from Tom. Tears of joy and smiles were on everyone's faces as they watched this beautiful scene unfold before them, a century in the making. After everyone regained control of their emotions they packed the remaining wagon and began to make their way out of the mountains.

Being down to one wagon and one extra horse, it made their travel slow. They took turns riding in the wagon and walking beside it. The group listened in comfortable silence that first day as Dr. Stein and Derian asked each other questions non-stop. There was nothing but joy about them, even when hearing the tragedies the other endured.

They listened as Derian told him about his connection to the lightning and the storm and how his skin changed tone due to his *touching the lightning*. Dr. Stein listened in fascination but still fussed over and examined Derian to make sure he was alright. Derian never once complained over his father's attention.

When camp was made that night stories from others finally began to be shared. Lucien told Dr. Stein everything that had happened since his escape.

"That is an incredible story Lucien. Graduated from the Citadel of the Martial, reconnected with your family, defeated Kane in single combat, and destroyed the 100 Blades, incredible," Dr. Stein said.

"And came and found me, and now has saved you," Derian interjected.

Dr. Stein squeezed his son's hand lovingly.

"What happened after I escaped Dr. Stein?" Lucien asked

"Truth be told Lucien, nothing much. A guard found me the next morning, still unconscious, he slapped me a few times to wake me up. I told the guard as if I was speaking to Igorrian that my slave killed the guards, assaulted me, and then escaped using the wrappings and armor of one of the dead guards. Igorrian shows up six days later to check on me. He seemed to be more in control of himself, less nervous or jittery. I asked what he was working on, and his response was, "Something that will change everything," and that was it, he left shortly thereafter and I never saw him again," Master Stein said.

"Between the vampires and Igorrian Al Saam there seems to be two enemies plotting something that cannot be good for the people of Arborreah," Lucien said.

"The kings will re-convene after the celebration in the Great Wood to discuss the vampire threat. Dr. Stein will you tell them the threat that this Igorrian Al Saam presents?" Timber asked.

"Of course. I want you all to know that I am in your debt. You all risked your lives for my son and I, and I will never forget this," Master Stein said.

"It was the right thing to do Dr. Stein. I think I can speak for all of us when I say you don't owe us anything," Tom said.

"I'm afraid young Thomas we'll just have to agree to disagree," Dr. Stein answered with a smile.

The next three days were slow but pleasant. On the morning of the fourth day the road split. This is where the main road south to Terramilene began. Before the horses could be pointed in the direction of their final destination Timber addressed the group.

"Benagar and I will be taking our leave of you now," Timber said.

All of the original travelers had shocked faces as they looked at the two veteran warriors.

"Oh, look at their faces Timber. We haven't even left yet, and they look lost already," Benagar said.

"Heh," Timber chuckled. "We've decided to go because with us gone no one would have to walk and you could make better time back to Terramilene. When we get to the city we will inform Prince Rory and I'm sure he will meet you with an escort. We will then head back to the Great Wood and brief your father on everything that has occurred. I speak for the both of us when I say it has been an honor and a privilege to share the road with all of you. To see such honor and courage in ones so young does our hearts good," Timber said.

"I feel I can speak for all of us when I say it's been *our* honor to share the road with legends such as yourselves. We will miss your wisdom," Lucien said.

"Wisdom? Maybe from Timber but all I saw from Benagar was that he was good at scaring stableboys," Quinn said with a smile.

"I'll see you at the Great Wood Prince Quinn where we will settle the bill," Benagar replied with a smile that told a story everyone knew; Quinn was going to have some pain coming his way.

Handshakes and hugs were exchanged knowing they would see each other in the Great Wood soon. The two handed their robes over to the twins, then jogged far enough away so as not to spook the horses, transformed into third form, and ran for Terramilene. The group watched the two run ahead for a bit before climbing into the wagon, Rob climbing on the extra horse and following after.

Two days out from Terramilene, Prince Rory, Sergeant Mason, and five other members of the Hammeraxe Legion met the group on the road.

"My Prince!" Lucien, Arissa, and the twins shouted.

Rory took his helmet off smiling and said, "You'll have to tell me how you escape the greetings of *Prince* each time you're in the company of friends Prince Quinn."

"Oh no I'll never tell," Quinn replied with a quick laugh.

"You must be Master Stein. It is an honor sir. Thank you for watching over Lucien, if not for you we may have never met him, and that would have been a shame as we've all grown quite fond of him," Rory said with a smile.

"The honor is all mine Prince Rory," Dr. Stein replied.

"And you must be Derian Stein. Well met Derian," Rory said.

" Well met Prince Rory," Derian replied.

"Please, in informal settings amongst friends as we all are, I would just be Rory."

"Thank you Rory," Derian said.

"Sergeant Mason, I think we've finally found someone who can at least match you in strength," Rory said.

"It would seem so my Prince," Sergeant Mason replied.

"What do you mean? Sergeant Mason has met me before. We will have that test of strength sir!" Quinn shouted.

"The prince should be careful what he wishes for," Sergeant Mason replied good naturedly.

Arissa saw Derian staring at the unicorns with childlike wonder.

"They're magnificent aren't they?" she asked.

"Truly. You hear about them and read about them, but to see them this close, it's amazing. Like a beautiful dream made flesh," Derian said.

"When we stop to camp, Rory will let you feed him," Arissa said.

"Really?"

"Of course. You're going to learn that Rory would do anything for his friends," Arissa said.

"If you are all not too weary, let us ride on," Rory instructed.

"No need for rest, we are ready for the city, baths and cold ale," Tom replied. Everyone agreed with him.

"Derian, please, follow me," Rory asked after the entire team made camp for the evening.

Derian and Rory strode to where the horses and unicorns were tied. Rory could sense the apprehension from the giant and stopped the two mid-stride.

"Brownie, my warhorse, has been with me since his birth. He trusts me more than most people, and for good reason. He knows I'd never bring someone, even of your size, to do him harm. He will accept you. If you can, relax and enjoy the moment. I do understand how intimidating it can be for those who have never seen one before," Rory shared.

The talk had the intended effect and the introduction of Derian and Brownie went smoothly. So easy was the connection that Rory returned to the campfire without the giant.

"Where's Derian?" Arissa asked.

"Brushing Brownie. As great a job the royal stable masters do with him, I doubt Brownie has had his muscles brushed so deeply. I think both of them are enjoying the moment," Rory replied to the group.

"Thank you Rory. To see that look of joy on my son's face is priceless," Dr. Stein said.

"Your son is now a part of this group of ours and with that comes some privileges," Rory said with a smile.

"I must thank you for something else. Lucien told me that you swore you would take up his quest to reunite me with my son if he fell against Kane. I don't know what to say, so much honor in all of you. It is humbling," Master Stein said.

"How about thanking my brother and I for exposing Derian to the best privilege of all, my brother and my eternal wit and charm," Rob said.

"Ha! Ha! He could do worse than that young ones. I have watched you all interact with him. No fear of his size, you all seem to have just naturally accepted him. I'll never be able to repay you all for this," Dr. Stein said.

"Master Stein there is nothing to repay. Your son has a good soul. We all knew early on that we had found another brother to add to our group," Lucien said.

"We will be at Terramilene soon and I worry about that. My son's past experience with people in Terramilene did not go well. I mean no disrespect Rory. Will you all watch him? I would hate to see him withdraw within himself if things do not go well," Dr. Stein said.

"We will watch him Dr. Stein, but I can assure you his time in Terramilene will be different this time," Rory said.

"Lucien and I have been talking about this very thing. The Great Wood is not as densely packed as Terramilene is and Derian wouldn't be greeted with fear. Awe and wonder, surely, but not fear. A home can be built for you both, and we can provide anything you need for a lab. You and Derian's name can be made known in Terramilene and we believe in time people will no longer be caught off guard by his size," Quinn said.

"I think it's a wonderful idea Prince Quinn," replied Dr. Stein.

"We thought so too didn't we Prince Quinn," Lucien said while jabbing his cousin in the ribs.

"Oh no don't try to get that started with me too," Quinn replied.

"The generosity you have all shown to my son and I.........I'm at a loss for words," Dr. Stein replied.

"If you feel you have to repay, I have an idea," Lucien said.

"Name it."

"Start to share your genius with others. Share it with those worthy of it," Lucien said.

"Well, I already planned on doing that but I think I know where I can direct my attention. You've both given me an idea," Dr. Stein said as he got up to tell Derian about their new home.

"That's a good thing you've done Quinn," Lucien said.

"I can't have you getting all the credit for everything around here," Quinn replied as he embraced Lucien in his usual bear-like hug.

"They're going to write songs about you Lucien," Tom said with pride for his friend.

"If all of your names aren't in them, I don't want to listen to them. Good night friends, family," Lucien replied.

He made his way to where Arissa was getting out their bedding and helped spread them out under the wagon.

Chapter Ten

"Lucien......Lucien."

"Derian? What is it?" Lucien asked as he came out of his asleep.

When travelling on the open road one learns to sleep lightly in case of danger, yet even with all his size Derian was able to move next to Lucien and awaken him without anyone being disturbed.

"Twenty men are moving on us from our backtrail," Derian said.

Lucien quickly joined Derian who was kneeling behind the wagon and staring in the direction they came from. Arissa and the twins were awake and alert. The twins nudged Quinn who was alert in seconds.

"I don't see them," Lucien said.

"They will be in range of your sight soon," Derian replied.

"Describe them," Lucien said.

"They left their horses behind to move in silence. They are all in black, when the moon is behind the clouds they move in the shadows as if they were made from darkness," Derian said.

"It is the Shadowmen. It appears they gave pursuit after all," Lucien said.

"They have come for my father. They will not have him," Derian said as he removed his massive hammer from the wagon. Lucien took note at the lack of noise in his gathering his weapon. If not for his size he could easily be one of the Shadowmen

"No, they will not. Keep watch while I alert the camp," Lucien said.

Lucien quickly but silently looked at his companions to see if they were at the ready. Arissa was up and inspecting her bow, the boys were alert and gave Lucien a nod, and Quinn transformed into third form, ran off to the side of the road and concealed himself. Lucien then went to Sergeant Mason and told him what was happening. He moved quickly and silently awakening the five other Legionnaires and Rory. Lucien was amazed at the quiet ease with which these big men moved. They were going to have to fight unarmored. They couldn't risk the moonlight reflecting off them and giving their position away. Within two minutes they were ready, laying on top of their hammeraxes and ready to spring their own surprise. Lucien made his way back to Derian and the others.

"Where are they now,?" Lucien asked.

"Closer. The next time the moon goes behind the clouds they will be upon us," Derian said.

"Lucien put on Claw and Fang across his back and then went under the wagon where Dr. Stein was sitting behind a wagon wheel.

"Take this Dr. Stein," Lucien said as he handed over a short sword that Rory gave him.

"We have taken the element of surprise and now we have it. Stay hidden doctor," Lucien said

"We move on your signal Derian," Lucien said.

The Shadowmen moved without a sound, black blades drawn, into the camp while the almost full moon was behind a cloud. It was covered for only a few moments before the cloud moved on.

"NOW!" Derian shouted and the battle was joined.

Derian moved from around the wagon with a speed not to be believed from a being his size. To see it in action was the only way to believe it, for no person or book could relay the action well enough.

"You'll not have my father again!" the giant screamed, the voice carrying well into the mountains.

With one swing of Derian's hammer, two Shadowmen went from alive and moving to dead and broken. Another intruder slipped to the side and sliced at the giant's legs. His blade missed Derian by inches. The giant used the momentum from his first swing to arc up and then directly down onto his opponent's head. The moon giving enough light to see a red mist wafting in the air.

Arissa fired arrows with her usual speed and deadly accuracy. She caught one Shadowman directly between the eyes as he was pushing forward to slam a spear into Derian's spine. She then turned attention to a collective group headed to the group of Legionnaire's and sliced through two more before she lost the light and had to pull back. She removed a short sword and retreated to where Dr. Stein hid, ready to give her life if an enemy attempted to abduct the elder.

The twins gained energy and power in their staves the faster they swung them. Quickly, standing back-to-back, they created an orb of death to three Shadowmen who knew nothing of the danger that awaited them. Another attempted to throw a spear at the twins only to have it cut into multiple pieces as it entered the whirlwind of death.

Quinn was tested in his patience as he let the entire group of men pass him, but when he confirmed they had all gone by without noticing his location he crept from behind and began tearing off limbs and ripping out throats. It was a gruesome and vicious attack, one that only wolves are able to conduct without remorse of any kind. He was able to get through four of them before they realized he was attacking from behind their ranks.

Rory and the Legionnaires were pressed. The Shadowman numbers overall had dwindled quickly but they still outnumbered the royal guards by almost two-to-one.

"Shields!" Rory ordered.

In unison the men made a shield wall that allowed them a defensive advantage. Clangs of metal on shields could be heard throughout the valley. Rory never faltered or hesitated in his duties as a captain and a man defending his friends. He would give a command and in perfectly timed harmony the shields would open from a section and Rory would step through and slice into an opponent, step back behind the shields and they would close in front of him. The choreograph of this dance was well executed but would have a difficult time sustaining based on numbers alone.

Lucien noted the disadvantage his friend was under and sprinted to equal the odds. He was only yards away when he witnessed the prince come from another pre-determined opening in the shield wall and split a man from shoulder to waist.

A Shadowman turned to face Lucien as he arrived. All thought left him as he settled his mind to the flow of his swords. The man he faced was skilled and put up a valiant battle but was bested by Lucien.

Lucien parried the man's sword with Claw, slide to his left while ducking the return swing of his opponent, then made a quick slice through the air and opened his opponents throat with Fang. The smell of blood filled the air and Lucien could feel all of his senses becoming more focused and his reactions quicker. It was as if he was becoming something else. He found the elite fighters from the desert land became slower and slower as he went from battle to battle. When his sight, hearing, strength and reflexes began to slow, and his heavy breathing could be felt on his chest, he looked around to see there were no more Shadowmen. Laying at his feet were seven that he had defeated himself.

"One of them is running back to the horses," Derian said looking back the way the Shadowmen had come.

"Where?" Arissa asked.

"He's too far away now little one," Derian said.

"Not for this bow. Please Derian direct my arm," Arissa asked.

Derian knelt down beside Arissa until his head was next to hers looking down the arrow she had already pulled back.

"Up a little, now over to the right. Alright hold, now loose," Derian said.

Arissa loosed. Derian stood and then looked down at Arissa with an amazed look on his face.

"You got him straight through the back of his head. A perfect shot," Derian said.

"We got him,' Arissa said.

"Is everyone alright?" Rory said.

"Private Wilson is down sir and in bad shape," Sergeant Mason said.

"Let me see him, bring torches," Dr. Stein said.

Private Wilson was on the ground, another Legionnaire pressing on a wound in Private Wilson's leg which was bleeding profusely.

"Please move away Legionnaire," Dr. Stein said to the man pressing on the wound.

"Bring that torch over here now," Dr. Stein said, a new firmness in his voice. "I need one of your stitching kits and I need it now. I need someone to hold a sharp blade to a flame as well."

Sergeant Mason was back in seconds with a standard Legionnaire stitching kit as every Legionnaire is trained to stitch minor wounds closed.

"Please give the private something to bite on for the pain. I'm going to open this wound a little so that I can sew the nick in the artery. Knife please," Dr. Stein said reaching his hand back without taking his eyes off of the private.

Arissa who had been heating one of her throwing knives in Rory's torch, immediately gave the blade to Dr. Stein, who then began to open the privates wound..

"Sergeant Mason I need you to pull on the private's thigh here to keep the wound open," Dr. Stein said.

Sergeant Mason did so, and the doctor took the already threaded needle from the kit and began. To the private's credit he refused something to bite on and he barely made a sound of any discomfort. Dr. Stein had the artery and the wound closed in a minute. The stitching was impeccable.

"You're going to be fine Private Wilson. Take it easy on that leg. No galloping and drink plenty of fluids. Give it a week before clipping those stitches," Dr. Stein said.

"Thank you Master Stein," Private Wilson said.

"You're welcome private."

"Thank you Dr. Stein, without you Wilson would be dead," Rory said.

"Think nothing of it Rory. A first-year student at the Citadel of the Mind could have done what I did. Although I admit being a bit out of practice. I should have had that procedure done much faster. Excuse me Rory I must check on Derian," Dr. Stein said.

"Of course," Rory replied thankful he wasn't going to have to visit Private Wilson's family to deliver terrible news.

Dr. Stein found Derian sitting down and cleaning blood from his hammer.

"How are you doing son?" Master Stein asked.

"Fine father, a few cuts that will be gone by morning," Derian replied.

"I mean how do you feel about the lives you took?" Master Stein asked.

Derian took a moment of thought then said, "They came to take you away from me again or kill you. They would have killed all of our new friends who are giving us freely a bright new future. I took no pleasure in killing them, but I also do not feel bad about their deaths, they made their choice."

Dr. Stein touched his son's face and smiled then went to see if anyone else needed medical attention.

The next hour was spent tending to minor wounds and cleaning weapons. The twins rode back and gathered up the Shadowmen's horses and gave them to Prince Rory to repay for the horses they had to leave behind on the outskirts of Oasis. Rory grudgingly took them as he did not feel there was anything to be repaid for. Say what you will but the horses were in fantastic condition and well taken care of. The dead were moved to the side of the road where time, animals, and elements would eventually get rid of them.

Arissa watched as Rory and Lucien had a quiet conversation which must have been a good one as they smiled, parted and Rory went to sleep near the Legionnaires and Lucien came over to her ready to salvage some of this night's sleep.

"What were you and Rory talking about?" Arissa asked.

"Oh nothing," Lucien said playfully.

"Tell me."

"It's a secret."

"Lucien Farrunner you can't keep secrets from me," Arissa said mildly annoyed.

"You'll find out after we reach the city," Lucien said.

"That's two days!" Arissa exclaimed.

"Quiet! People are trying to sleep," Quinn shouted.

"You're one to talk Quinn Farrunner. We'll be lucky if your snoring doesn't wake the Shadowmen and we have to fight them all over again!" Arissa shouted back.

"I don't snore," Quinn said under his breath.

"Good night Arissa," Lucien said as he kissed her on the cheek and closed his eyes.

"Before you fall asleep. I saw you change tonight. What happened?" Arissa asked in the darkness.

"What do you mean?" Lucien asked.

"I was protecting Dr. Stein and saw you fighting four men at one time and none of them could get near you. Your speed and precision was like nothing I've ever seen from you, or anyone else. It was as if you were someone, or something, else. It was both fascinating and frightening. Four men at once Lucien. No one survives that," Arissa whispered. There was a sincere concern in her voice.

"I don't know. I just focused on fighting and not what might happen if I lost. Everything did seem to slow down for me, but I think it was only adrenaline.," Lucien said.

Arissa stopped asking question and stared at the night sky for a bit, annoyed, but eventually leaned into Lucien, kissed his cheek, and fell asleep.

The next two days on the road were pleasant and uneventful, full of laughing and good natured ribbing as only close friends can do. They entered Terramilene without fanfare as was found after defeating the 100 Blades. Many people recognized Rory and random people would call out, "Prince Rory!" and wave to him. Rory would smile and wave back. There were shouts of, "Farrunner!" as well, and even the twins and Arissa heard their names called out. Soon they were all waving. One older woman came up to the slow-moving wagon and gave Arissa flowers. Arissa blushed, a little embarrassed at the attention, but she smiled and thanked the old woman.

Prince Rory relieved the five Legionnaires of duty and told private Wilson to get some rest. Sergeant Mason, as always, remained by the prince's side. Many young women lined the streets and called out to the twins and Quinn and of course the boys loved the attention.

Two teens walked up to the wagon, looked at Derian, then walked next to Rory and asked, "Prince Rory have you captured a giant?"

Rory looked down smiled and said, "No, that is Derian Stein our friend and brother and newest hero of the realm."

The boys looked back at Derian in the wagon. Their eyes wide in wonderment.

"Hello lads," Derian said in that deep rumbling, but soothing voice of his.

The boys smiled and waved goodbye clearly overjoyed at meeting the prince and his heroic friends. They ran off to tell their friends and family all about meeting a real-life giant.

Arissa leaned back from the driver's seat she shared with Lucien and said, "Something tells me Dr. Stein your son's reception by the people of Terramilene will be much better now than in times past."

"I believe you may be right my dear," Dr. Stein replied as he looked across at his smiling son.

The procession made their way through the city. Ahead of them a large group of people gathered. As they grew nearer to the crowd they saw the gallows and the three men upon it, the crier, the hangman, and the guilty. When they were parallel across from the gallows Arissa pulled the reins for the wagon to stop. Lucien called for Rory who was ahead of the wagon to stop. Arissa stood up on the driver's seat and looked at the accused. It was then Lucien recognized who was being hanged. Skinny Pete. The one who "greeted" them and was rude, to put it mildly, to Arissa when they found the 100 Blades. Lucien told this to Rory and Sergeant Mason.

Rob leaned over to the Steins and Quinn from his horse to the wagon and said, "This particular member of the 100 Blades made the mistake of touching Arissa and speaking to her in, shall we say, an inappropriate manner."

The crier continued to read from a ledger, reciting Pete's long list of crimes. Pete just stood there. He didn't cry or beg for mercy. He just stood there with the defeated look of a man who was about to meet his end.

Arissa continued to stare daggers at him while they were stopped on the road. At some point Pete looked up and he and Arissa's eyes met. There was a look of recognition in Pete's eyes that Arissa returned with a smile that was full of mean spirit. The crier finished reading Pete's crimes and asked if he had anything to say. Pete just shook his head. The hangman pulled the lever, the trapdoor opened, Pete dropped, his neck snapped, and that was it. Arissa watched a little longer than the rest of the group then sat down. Lucien snapped the reins and the friends moved on into the city.

Prince Rory directed the group through the city until he came to the front of a building where they could tie up the unicorns and the wagon team. The sign outside of the large building read: Tailor.

Prince Rory led them inside where they were greeted by a finely dressed older gentleman.

"Prince Rory! I didn't know you were coming. To what do I owe this pleasure?" the man asked.

"Hello Terrence. My apologies. It was kind of a spur of the moment idea, but you have said you enjoy a challenge," Rory said.

"Indeed I do. What have you brought for me today?" Terrence asked.

"Terrence I would like you to meet Master of the Citadel of the Mind, Dr. Francis Nigel Stein and his son Derian Stein."

"Master Stein it is a pleasure, and you, Derian, step forward so I can get a better look at you," Terrence said smiling up into Derian's face.

"Hello sir," Derian said shyly.

"Please, Terrence, and don't you worry young man there is no one, no matter what the size, that I can't make fine clothing for," Terrence said.

"Thank you sir, uh Terrence, but I have no money to pay you with," Derian replied.

"The crown will be covering all expenses," Rory cut in.

"Prince Rory you've already done so much for my son and I," Dr. Stein started.

"Master Stein think nothing of it. You and Derian need clothes. Besides you and Derian won't be the only ones getting fitted today. Terrence let me introduce…" Rory started.

"Please, my prince, what kind of citizen of Terramilene would I be if I didn't know the young heroes who destroyed the 100 Blades. Robert and Thomas Hollis, and this beautiful young lady is Arissa. Will Prince Quinn and his equally famous cousin Lucien be getting fitted as well?" Terrence asked.

"I think Prince Quinn and Lucien are fine, but yes these three will need to be fitted as well," Rory said.

"Rory what are you doing?" Arissa asked.

"Listen, if I am going to keep being seen with all of you I can't very well have people asking why are my friends are so scruffy, or why do they keep seeing you in the same clothes," Rory said with a wink and a smile.

"So, Terrence, we're going to need the full compliment. Formal wear, travel wear, boots, formal and travel as well, smallclothes, everything," Rory said.

"Of course my prince. Olivia, Bernard, Phillip, Susan, come out here please, and bring the stepladder as well," Terrence said with a quick two claps.

Four apprentices came from a back room, bowed before Rory and introduced themselves to the others. To their credit none of them reacted indecently to Derian's size or to the fact that the shop was full of royalty and heroes. Everyone who was receiving clothes was led to the back to begin being measured.

"This is a fine thing you are doing Rory," Lucien said.

"It's nothing," Rory replied.

"All I know is you are making me look bad," Quinn said.

"Quinn if I know you and your family and the celebration that is waiting for you all when you get home, they won't even remember this," Rory said as he pat Quinn's back.

An elaborate carriage surrounded by royal guardsmen on horseback stopped outside the shop. Rory, Quinn, and Lucien watched through the shop front windows as a footman opened the carriage door and helped the queen exit the carriage. The king followed, needing no help.

Sergeant Mason went to them and saluted, and the boys could see he was giving them a full report on their journey. They could tell he was telling them about the attack by the Shadowmen because the king's face grew angry, and his fists clenched while the queen's face grew worried and concerned. Sergeant Mason finished his report and then held the door for them to enter the shop. The boys bowed and greeted the king and queen. The queen went to Rory and started fussing over him, asking if he was alright.

"I'm fine mother,' Rory said.

"Quinn, Lucien is everyone alright?" King Willem asked.

"Yes your majesty. We are all fine thank you. How did you know we were here?" Quinn asked.

"What kind of king and queen would we be if we didn't know where our son was in our own city," King Cromwell replied with a wink and a smile.

"Your majesties! You honor me by my visiting my shop." Terrence exclaimed.

"Nonsense Terrence, it has been too long since the king and I have visited," the queen replied.

The Steins had finished their fitting and made their way from the back of the store to see the king and queen. Rory walked over to them.

"Dr. Stein, Derian, allow me to introduce you to my parents, King Willem and Queen Gwendolyn Cromwell."

"Your majesties," the Steins said together. Dr. Stein bowed while Derian just moved his head some as there was no room for him to make the formal movement.

"Dr. Stein, Derian, from the moment Lucien told us your story, my wife and I have been waiting to meet the both of you. On behalf of the crown and the people of Terramilene you both have our sincerest apologies. You were taken from our city in the dead of night and were treated poorly and driven away. These things will never happen again I assure you both, "The king said.

"Your majesties there is nothing to forgive. These things happened long ago. Through the honor of these young heroes, including your son, I have my son back. Your son has been kind and generous and brave. I know you are proud of him," said Master Stein.

"We are. We were told you saved a Legionnaires life, we are eternally grateful," The Queen said.

"It was nothing your majesty."

"We were also told you would be modest," The queen replied.

"If there is anything the crown can do for you or your son Master Stein do not hesitate to ask," The king said.

"Actually, your majesty there is," Dr. Stein said.

"Name it."

"I am a tenured master at the citadel, but since I have been gone for so long I may need a royal writ to assure them that I am indeed who I say I am," Dr. Stein said.

"All will be taken care of in that regard whenever you return to the citadel," The king replied.

"Thank you your majesty."

"Quinn, please ask your father when he would like to sit down and discuss the imminent threats that are looming over our peoples. Prince Rory can relay his answer to me when he returns," The king said.

"When I return. From where father?" Rory asked.

"From the Great Wood of course. A celebration is awaiting the heroes who destroyed the 100 Blades. I believe you are one of those heroes and Terramilene must be represented at this celebration. Take the good sergeant with you," The king said.

"Thank you father," Rory said exchanging smiles with his father.

The others were finished being measured and joined everyone at the front of the store.

"The king and I are overjoyed to see you all returned safely," The queen said.

"Thank you your majesty," The twins and Arissa replied.

"Well, we've held you all up long enough. I'm sure your family worries every second you're not home. Safe travels young ones," the king said.

"Terrence it's been a pleasure but we must take our leave," Prince Rory said.

"The pleasure is all mine Prince Rory. This order will take top priority. Safe travels," Terrence said as he waved goodbye.

"I take it that was the surprise you were keeping from me?" Arissa asked Lucien as they readied the wagon for the road.

"That it was," Lucien said.

"We have wonderful friends don't we?" Arissa asked.

"We certainly do," Lucien replied.

No time was spent in the city, the entire group made their way for the Farrunners home in the Great Woods.

Chapter Eleven

For two days Dr. Stein used their travel time to question Quinn about how werewolves transformed, if any pain was felt, how long one could go without transforming, or stay transformed and if Quinn, or any other werewolf, felt differently while transformed, among many other questions.

Quinn, one to enjoy as much attention as he could get, answered every question thrown his way, and added quite a few details the Dr. had not even thought to ask. Lucien was thankful for Quinn's willingness to be all but interrogated as there were some pieces of information shared that Lucien didn't know either.

When there was any quiet pauses, or moments of reflection from the Dr., Quinn would remind everyone about the celebration that was awaiting them.

"Expect a wild time. There is going to be music, dancing, more food than you can fathom and of course enough ale to drown an army!" Quinn would share.

"Here, my friends, is the entrance to the Great Wood," Quinn said to Dr. Stein and Derian as they entered into his family's kingdom.

"Beautiful," Dr. Stein stated in nothing more than a whisper. His eyes were almost as wide as his mouth as the natural magic of the canopy enveloped him.

"Father, do you hear the songbirds? Have you ever heard ones sing like that?" Derian asked.

"Those are Flickerlocks. Legend has it they were the first living things to make the Great Wood their home and still sing the songs of the old days. The only time they have a different song, or noise, is when we howl while in third form. They have learned to mimic our howling. It turns the entire Great Wood into a harmonic symphony on those nights," Quinn shared.

The majestic ways of the Great Wood wasn't only affecting Dr. Stein and Quinn. All but Quinn were comforted with a blanket of joy as they made their way closer to Quinn's home. Arissa rested her head on Lucien's shoulder as they rode, a peaceful and content smile sitting on their faces. The only two not still were the two newest to the land. They continually looked around, trying to consume the entire forest at one time.

"Your home is beautiful Quinn," Derian said as he pointed to a handful of deer lazily eating near the road.

"It is you and your father's home too now," Quinn replied.

Derian sat back again, now trying to visualize himself in this land and what it would be like to travel on his own in such a magnificent place. He couldn't wait to explore all the land had to offer.

"Scouts have gone ahead and told of our coming," Quinn called out.

It was when the group was approximately half a mile from the city where the first chants came to their ears.

"Farrunner! Farrunner! Farrunner!" Was cried out over and over again.

When the wagons turned to the clearing at the entrance of the city the sound was all but deafening. It would be easy to think every living soul had gathered along the sides of the main road to greet the returning heroes. The

Farrunner chants and cheers seemed to grow louder with each step the horses made toward the center of the city.

When the group thought it couldn't be any louder, Quinn stood in the back of the wagon and raised his fist in triumph. The accompanying result was another notch higher in the decibels of noise due to the crowd erupting in cheers at their prince's return.

Quinn screamed at Arissa and Lucien as he dropped down from his wagon. Lucien shook his head, not understanding what his cousin was saying as the prince bound up the wagon, but Arissa took the reins and shoved Lucien into his cousin as Quinn boarded their wagon.

Quinn took Lucien's hand and raised it with his own. The crowd went wild at the sight of the conquering duo. Many of those in attendance sang out *LU-CIEN, LU-CIEN, LU-CIEN.*

Lucien waved Rob and Tom off their horses and into the back of the wagon with them. The twins needed no prompting, jumped up and threw their hands in the air as well. The crowd cheered them all as tales of their heroics had reached the whole of the Great Wood. As the twins were waving at the sea of people, two young women caught their eye. It was their friends from the last time they visited the Great Wood. The boys looked at each other, a different type of excitement in their eyes, then pointed at the girls and then motioned to the castle, trying to indicate they would meet the young ladies at the final stopping point.

Dr. Stein understood how important this moment was, had Derian take the reins of the wagon he was in, climbed next to Arissa, took the reins from her, smiled and motioned for her to join the boys. She kissed him on the cheek and jumped in the back of the wagon. Lucien was feeding off the energy of the crowd and without thinking, bent down and made Arissa sit on his shoulders. The crowd went ecstatic and almost delirious at the sight of the young human woman raised high into the air, who showed more courage and bravery than any they had ever heard of. The cheers for her were deafening. There wasn't an individual in the crowd who wasn't waving and smiling.

Finally, the procession reached the steps leading to castle Wolfhearth where the royal family, Master Jerron, Timber, and Benagar awaited. Attendants came and led the horse and wagon teams away to private stables reserved for guests. Prince Rory and Sergeant Mason dismounted, leaned their heads against their unicorns, and spoke words of ease. The words would calm the steeds and allow the waiting attendants to lead the unicorns away without issue, as a unicorn does not easily get separated from its owner when in a new place.

When Derian got out of the wagon there were some expressions of awe but not fear. The group began walking toward the royal family led by Quinn and Lucien. Master Stein and Derian hanging toward the back to wait to be introduced. There were plenty of hugs and handshakes. Queen Sera shed tears of joy and relief that all were safe. Brienne and William gave crushing embraces to all. Timber and Benagar had smiles for the group and Master Jerron told everyone how happy he was to see them all again safe and sound. The king was a picture of beaming pride. His hugs had everyone gasping for air and Rory felt the king's embrace even through his armor. Quinn then turned and motioned for Dr. Stein and Derian to come forward.

"Father, mother, William, Brienne, Master Jerron, this is Master Francis Nigel Stein and his son Derian Stein. I told them they could make their home here in the Great Wood," Quinn said.

"Master Stein, my nephew shared the amazing and sad story both you and your son has endured. You took care of my nephew while you were both enslaved, and you helped him escape. The kingdom of the Great Wood and my family can never repay you for this. It would be our honor if you and your son would call the Great Wood your home. No expense of material or strong backs will be spared in the creation of whatever type of home suits your wants and needs. Details will be discussed later. For now, welcome both of you," King Killian said.

Both Steins bowed and thanked the king. The king then began to address the people.

"Wolves of the Great Wood your sons have returned!" King Killian said while gesturing to Quinn and Lucien.

He waited for the cheering to subside before continuing. The king gestured to the twins and Arissa to stand next to him and his queen.

"They return with these other young heroes. All of them walked into the hidden camp of the 100 Blades where my nephew defeated Kane in single hand-to-hand combat!"

The chant of "Lucien!" arose from the crowd. When it subsided the king continued, "The next day my son led the Hammeraxe Legion, led by Prince Rory Cromwell, to the 100 Blades camp and smashed them utterly, killing most and apprehending the rest."

Now the chant of "Cromwell" came from the masses.

The king continued, "Was that enough? No. After turning the rest of the 100 Blades over to King Cromwell for justice to be served, my nephew led another dangerous mission into the faraway land of Kabaal. This mission was to free the man who took care of him while he was enslaved there."

This time growls of anger came from the crowd.

"Once again these young heroes triumphed and rescued this man and reunited him with his son. These two new friends of the Great Wood stand before you now, Master Francis Nigel Stein and his son Derian Stein!" the king shouted.

Stein shouts rang from the crowd. When these ended the king went on, "Now, we will let these heroes wash the road from themselves and get a little rest before tonight's celebration!"

With that final roar of the crowd the king turned and led everyone inside castle Wolfhearth. They all stepped inside the large throneroom for a more personal reunion. Embraces and smiles started again. When they finished Quinn and Lucien stood before the king.

"Father we must tell you something," Quinn said.

"What is it?" the king asked.

"We were attacked two days out from Terramilene on the road by 20 Shadowmen," Quinn stated.

"What!?" the king replied as his entire demeanor changed. The smell of intense anger came off of him in waves. He tilted his head back towards Timber and Benagar.

"My king it was my call to leave them on the road at the time we did. I thought it was the right decision. If there is to be punishment, it should fall on me alone," Timber said.

The king took in a breath and looked as if he was going to begin shouting at one of his oldest friends when Lucien cut in.

"No uncle if Timber and Benagar didn't leave when they did then Prince Rory and his five Legionnaires wouldn't have been there, and we would have been more outnumbered than we were, and someone may have died. If not for Dr. Stein's incredible skill, one of those Legionnaires would have."

"Well done Master Stein," Queen Sera said.

"Twas nothing. A first-year surgical student could have saved the lad," Dr. Stein replied.

"Excuse me sir but I will hear no more of that," a firm voice spoke from behind the group.

"We were all there and Private Wilson's wound was mortal. I can speak for us all when I say the speed and precision of the stitching was beyond skilled. Private Wilson is a good lad and his future as a Legionnaire is bright and because you were there, you sir! Prince Rory and I did not have to tell his parents that their son was dead, that he died with honor, but still dead, nonetheless. You may not have swung a sword or slain an enemy, but you are every bit the hero any of us are. Please sir, if you wish to continue to downplay what you did, make sure I am not within earshot because I would not hear it again," Sergeant Mason said.

"Well said!" The twins shouted at once.

Everyone stood there in amazement. This is the most any of them have ever heard the sergeant say at one time. Dr. Stein walked over to him.

"Sergeant Mason will you give me your first name?" Dr. Stein asked.

"Graham sir."

"Thank you, Graham," Dr. Stein said and extended his hand which Sergeant Mason took and the two men shook in mutual respect.

"It seems the vampires are not the only ones who have a reckoning coming. This Igorrian al Saam will become a problem if left unchecked won't he Dr. Stein?" King Killian asked.

"Most assuredly your highness," Master Stein said.

"King Killian, my father requests that a meeting between the two of you after the celebration ends would probably be wise," Prince Rory said.

"Your father is correct, but, like he said, that is for after the celebration. You all will be taken to your rooms where you can wash and rest. Fresh clothes will be waiting for you all. Derian, I am sorry, but we do not have clothes in your size yet, but leave yours in your room when you bathe and we will have them cleaned. You will not fit in the tub, but the water will be hot and soap will be there along with plenty of towels. We also put four beds together for you, just don't jump on them," the king said with a smile. "I already have my craftsmen and tailor on these things. They will custom make all the things you need. I do not know that timeline, but they are working on it as we speak."

"Thank you for your generosity King Killian, but Prince Rory took us to Terrrence's and had us fitted for clothing," Derian said.

"Terrence is the best father, but I think we can provide something for Derian," Princess Brienne said. She then whispered something in her mother's ear.

The Queen smiled and said, "That is a wonderful idea Brienne."

"Alright off with you all, someone will come get you in a few hours for tonight's celebration," the king said.

"Master Stein, a moment please." Master Jerron stated as the individuals dispersed.

"Yes, Master Jerron."

"I would very much like to speak with you later. Lucien shared with us your story. Your long life and your amazing son, it would be my honor to talk with you and share ideas," Master Jerron said.

"The honor is mine Master Jerron, in fact there is something I would like to discuss with you. An idea I have been thinking about that you in fact are uniquely suited to provide me with the proper perspective on," Master Stein replied.

"I look forward to it, later then," Master Jerron replied as the two shook hands.

The group met a few hours later in the throneroom clean and rested. Except for the twins. They were clean and while they didn't necessarily look tired, they did look worn out. The men and women were dressed similarly. The men wore loose shirts, trousers and boots. The women also with loose shirts, loose flowing skirts and flat sandals. The material for all the clothing was light to allow for the night air of the Great Wood to keep them cooler as they danced and celebrated. Even though Derian wore the same clothes, after a thorough cleaning, they looked brand new. Timber, Benagar, and Sergeant Mason, though dressed for celebration, were still armed with short swords. Servants opened the large front doors of the castle and the group walked out to an amazing scene. Evening had come to the Great Wood, but light was everywhere. Colored streamers adorned the trees. There were benches and bonfires everywhere. There were many stalls set up selling all manner of food and drink. Fantastic smells filled the air. Sweets for the children and kegs of ale were all about. Musicians were playing tunes that kept everyone smiling and lively. People were everywhere and when they saw the royal family and guests emerge from the castle the people cheered and raised up whatever they were drinking to toast them.

"Wolves of the Great Wood, before this celebration gets started, if you make your way to the stage, the Hollis twins, Rob and Tom, will re-enact the fight between my nephew Lucien and Kane of the 100 Blades," the king announced.

The crowd cheered and began to make their way to the stage area where rows of low benches were waiting for the spectators. Even when all the seats were filled, people stood and sat where they could. No one wanted to miss the performance. When everyone was settled the twins leaped upon the stage, waved to the cheering crowd, and began to re-enact this fight that they had performed a few times now. The crowd was silent as they hung on every word and watched every move performed.

Those that had watched each performance agreed the one performed that night was the best one yet. When Kane was *killed* the crowd went crazy and started chanting "Lucien! Lucien! Lucien!" The boys started waving for Lucien to join them onstage. Lucien was in the front row and was reluctant to join the twins as he was a little shy at the attention, but Arissa shoved him off his seat and he joined the twins where they quickly embraced each other. Lucien turned to the crowd before him and despite his shyness began to speak.

"The story doesn't end there though good people," Lucien said.

Lucien then told the people everything that happened after that. How the next day after the Hammeraxe Legion battlehorn sounded and Arissa slew Billy the Beast with an arrow to the eye. How the twins slew two more of the 100 Blades. How Prince Quinn was first to leap into the infamous mercenary band ripping and tearing. How Prince Rory and the Legion rode in on their fabled steeds, armor gleaming in the sun, and smashed the100 Blades. Lucien called his friends up on the stage where they all embraced and the crowd went wild. Prince Rory looked over towards where Sergeant Mason was standing with Timber and Benagar to call him up on stage as the good sergeant was just a part of this story as anyone else on that stage. The sergeant put his hand up politely declining as if to say that this was the Prince's time.

The king came onstage and hugged each one of them. Once the last person was squeezed to the point of losing air from their lungs, the king turned to the crowd, threw his arms up and shouted, "Let the celebration begin!"

The minstrels struck up a lively tune and the celebration started in earnest, everyone mingling, laughing, and dancing.

"We're going to get some ale, does anyone want, OOF!" Rob started before he and Tom were almost bowled over by Priya and Mara jumping into their arms and covering them with kisses. The girls were telling them how impressed they were at their courage and strength. The twins walked off with the girls. The others in the group thought it odd at how it seemed they weren't as excited to see each other as they should have been. It was almost like this wasn't the first time they were seeing the other since leaving the Great Wood.

"Guess we'll be getting our own ale," Quinn said laughing.

Someone else who garnered immediate attention was Derian Stein. There seemed to be equal amounts of children and beautiful women around him. The children and Derian laughed as they climbed on him and he played with them, carrying them around and throwing them in the air. As playful as he was with the children, he was equally courteous and charming with the women who were obviously interested in play of a different kind. Derian's dance card was filled for the rest of the evening.

"Master Stein, where did Derian learn to dance or speak to women with such….skill?" Quinn asked.

"I wish I could take credit. I taught him the basics of both, but this, I guess comes naturally," Master Stein answered.

"I guess I better find my dance partner for the night before Derian scoops them all up," Quinn said.

"You will be as respectful as Derian is. Isn't that right Quinn?" Queen Sera stated more than asked.

"Yes mother," Quinn replied as he walked off.

Hours went by with the companions being pulled in one direction or another. People wanting to buy them drinks or thank them for everything they did. Prince Rory and Sergeant Mason were standing off to the side with the same glass of wine they started the evening with. Prince Rory didn't like the feeling of being drunk and he didn't want to do anything embarrassing that would disappoint his parents. Sergeant Mason had to keep his wits and senses alert to keep a watchful eye on his prince. The two of them were joking together when Quinn interrupted them.

"Sergeant Mason! You have avoided me long enough. It's time you prove your mettle!" Quinn shouted.

Prince Rory and Sergeant Mason walked over to where Quinn was waiting by two seats and a table designed for the age-old test of strength, the arm wrestle. Quinn was sitting down on one end.

"Are you sure Prince Quinn? We are here in front of your family, friends, and people," Sergeant Mason asked.

"Please, sir I've been waiting for this since I've heard the stories of your legendary strength. Give me your best.," Quinn replied.

"Alright then," the sergeant said after a deep sigh.

Bets began to fly back and forth, most putting their money on the taller and seemingly bigger Quinn. It was agreed that calling upon the power of the wolf was not allowed. This stipulation didn't change the betting at all. Prince Quinn was the heavy favorite. Prince William joined Prince Rory.

"How about it Prince Rory, 20 gold pieces my brother beats your Sergeant Mason?"

"Prince William you are on," Rory replied.

The two settled into their seats across from each other. Each one grabbing a peg in opposite corners of the table to steady themselves. They locked hands and locked eyes. A referee came out of the crowd and made sure their hands were locked together evenly. When all was set a silence blanketed the crowd and the anticipation was released when the referee raised his hands while yelling, *GO!*

Prince Quinn put all his considerable strength into beating Sergeant Mason quickly…..to no avail. It was as if the sergeant was made of stone. He didn't move one iota. Sweat broke out on Quinn's face and still the sergeant didn't move. Finally, the sergeant began to slowly move Prince Quinn's arm down. Quinn strained with everything he had, but his hand just kept moving down until finally it was over, and Quinn was beaten. Sounds of disappointment came from the crowd of onlookers as most lost their money. There was a loud cheer from Prince Rory who collected his winnings from Prince William. There were many who came to challenge Sergeant Mason after that, and all met the same end. Defeat. The good sergeant barely broke a sweat, and Prince Rory's winnings kept growing. When it seemed there would be no more challengers the sergeant went to get up from the table when someone else spoke.

"Good sir if you aren't too tired there is one more challenger," the voice was Timber's and the challenger was Benagar.

"I believe I have enough for one more," Sergeant Mason replied.

The two settled in at the table not taking their eyes off of each other. Their faces said the same thing, "Finally a challenge". The crowd seemed to sense this as well as the bets flew intensely. The odds were three to one against the sergeant because Benagar was so fresh not because of the size difference, after defeating opponent after opponent, all who were larger than the sergeant, the crowd realized it wasn't size that mattered. A hush settled in as the referee readied their hands. Once again he said *GO!*

The crowd erupted at that, most cheering for the legendary Benagar Winterspath, but there were quite a few cheers for Sergeant Mason after watching him defeat challenger after challenger for over an hour. For the first time real effort showed on the face of Sergeant Mason and soon both opponents were sweating with the strain. Finally, after 15 minutes of very little movement, Benagar's arm finally started to go down to the amazement of the crowd and when he was defeated, much of the crowd cheered in respect of the sergeant's incredible strength. Benagar took the sergeant's wrist and lifted his arm in victory as a sign of respect which was a good thing because Sergant Mason himself didn't think he could raise his arm himself. The crowd began to quiet down as a tall stunning woman came walking towards Sergeant Mason.

"Who's that?" Rory asked William.

"That's the lady Lucretia. She is the Great Wood's foremost herbalist. She knows more about plants and their healing properties than anyone. Even Master Jerron consults her from time to time. She's very respected and a little scary," William said.

"What do you mean?" Rory asked.

"Well she's very…..stern. She brooks no fools and when she speaks, she expects you to listen. Do not make her repeat herself," William replied

Lucretia made her way to Sergeant Mason and stood before him with a jar in her hands.

"I am Lucretia. Please remove your shirt Sergeant Mason. I have an ointment that will help ease the discomfort in your arm," she said.

Sergeant Mason gingerly removed his shirt and the crowd reacted with nods and expressions of understanding why he went unbeaten. Underneath the sergeant's loose shirt was a torso, chest, shoulders and arms that were all muscle. It was as if he was carved from a single piece of stone.

Those in the immediate area of Lucretia and Sergeant Mason were greeted with a pleasant smell when the herbalist opened the jar. She scooped a liberal amount from the container. She then began to rub the ointment into the sergeant's right shoulder, right arm and down the upper part of his back. Everyone watching the woman work her medicinal magic could tell the ointment was having an almost immediate effect as the sergeant's face relaxed with each new muscle that received attention.

"Before you turn in for the evening come find me as you will need more applied before you sleep. You will most likely find me speaking with Masters Jerron and Stein. There is something they are very excited about, and they say they need my expertise," Lucretia said.

"I will m'lady," Sergeant Mason replied.

At that moment Princess Brienne came storming over to where her brother and Rory were standing.

"Oooohhh she looks mad. Wonder what you did?" William said.

"Rory Cromwell! I have been waiting all night for you to ask me to dance!" the princess said very loudly looking up into Rory's face.

"Princess I…I…" Rory stammered.

"Come on!" she said as she took Rory by the hand and pulled him to the dancefloor.

Rory had one last look over his shoulder and saw William laughing and waving goodbye to him. Next thing he knew he was turning and spinning with Brienne as the musicians played a jaunty tune. The two were soon smiling as the princess' early anger with Rory disappeared and they enjoyed dancing together. The song ended and a slower one began. Dance partners drew closer to each other for a more intimate time. Princess Brienne put her arms around Rory's neck and looked up into his face smiling. Rory met her eyes and for the first time really saw her as the beautiful young woman she had become. It was then that Lucien and Arissa danced their way over to them.

"You were right Brienne, he does dance well," Arissa said with a big enough smile for the both of them.

"I told you," Brienne replied.

As Lucien and Arissa danced away from them Rory watched them and said," Your cousin is the most honorable man I know."

Princess Brienne took her finger, put it on Rory's chin and turned his face back to hers and said, "My cousin is not the only one with honor."

She then went up on her toes and kissed him on the corner of his mouth and then rested her head on his chest as they danced, leaving Prince Rory with his head swirling.

Chapter Twelve

Rory awoke the next morning refreshed and ready to enjoy a training session with his friends. After he did a quick wash of his face and dressed he made his way for the door. Just before walking out, he grabbed the large leather pouch. It was considerably heavier at the end of the night than the beginning. It should though, as it contained all the gold coin from the bets he made while Sergeant Mason arm wrestled.

As prince Cromwell walked through the hallway, swinging the pouch, he was happy to give the entire contents to his most trusted advisor. It was not long ago the King told Rory that Sergeant Mason would be by his side night and day. As most young people wanting their freedom would, Rory protested but it fell on deaf ears. There was no negotiation with his father that would allow the prince to keep from having the sergeant next to him.

Now that time has passed, Rory could not imagine last night's arm-wrestling champion not being by his side. Above the perfectly timed advice, or knowing when to let Rory make the mistake so he could learn, or giving guidance on how to lead, and above the long conversations no one else would ever be privy to, it was the fact that Sergeant Mason respected Rory as a person. That is worth more than any bag of gold could ever buy.

Rory gave an easy rap on the sergeant's door. Shuffling and muffled voices were heard from behind it. When the door was unlatched and opened, Lady Lucretia was standing there. Rory smiled and stood aside to allow her to leave.

"Good morning, Prince Rory," she said, after passing through the threshold of Sergeant Mason's room.

"Good morning, Lady Lucretia," Rory replied.

Rory watched the herbalist walk off, carrying herself with pride even though her hair was a little out of place. Rory entered the sergeant's room with a big knowing smile on his face. The sergeant was putting on his swordbelt, the smell of the lady's ointment for Sergeant Mason's arm filled the room.

"Good morning sergeant," Rory exclaimed

"Uh, good morning my prince," the sergeant replied.

"I'm glad to see the Lady Lucretia continued to care for your…..arm. How does it feel?" Rory said.

"Perfectly fine my prince. The Lady Lucretia is very skilled," Sergeant Mason replied.

"I'm sure. Here is your half of the winnings from last night," Rory said as he placed the heavy pouch on the sergeant's nightstand.

"Not necessary my prince,"

"Yes it is. You earned it, don't make me order you to take it," Rory said.

"Thank you my prince," Sergeant Mason said as he picked up the bag to place it in a more secure location. He bounced the bag in his large hand a couple of times and said, "This is a *little* more than half."

"Consider it a bonus. No arguing," Rory explained.

"Sir…"

Ignoring his sergeant, Rory turned to face the open door and said, without looking back, "Alright let's go meet the others."

The two men walked out of the sergeant's room when the two doors to the twin's rooms opened simultaneously. Priya and Mara exited into the hallway smiling and giggling.

"Oh, good morning Prince Rory, Sergeant Mason," the girls said, attempting to gather some form of decorum.

"Good morning Priya. Good morning Mara," Rory replied.

The girls exited quickly. As the last of their backs could be seen Rob and Tom came into the hallway, ready for practice.

"Well good morning you two. I hope you got enough rest for this morning's practice," Rory said.

"Don't worry about us, you worry about yourself not ending up on your back this morning," Rob replied.

Rory laughed and the four men continued down the hall. Before they got to Lucien's room, his door opened and out came Arissa and Lucien, laughing and smiling.

"Ah and here are the last two members of our group. I hope you two got enough rest," Tom said with a sarcastic smile.

"Worry about yourself," Arissa replied as she delivered a playful elbow to Tom's ribs.

"I hope you're all ready for a punishing practice session," Lucien said.

"It's been too long," Rob stated.

The group agreed that it had.

After practice everyone separated for some time away from the constant *go* they had been enduring over the last twenty-four hours.

Lucien returned to his room, alone, and after washing spent the next few hours in his room writing Ben and Martha.

The long letter detailed all that had happened in his life since he left them. He spared no situation. Some of the gruesome details he thought better of jotting down, but he shared both the good and the bad. He told them who he and his family and people really were and why they had such secrecy. He told them he loved them and missed them and hoped to visit soon.

Tom went to Rob's room and the twins wrote to their parents, telling them all that has been occurring in their lives, and that they would write again soon.

Arissa and Brienne went to the dressing room which Arissa didn't care for but enjoyed for the sake of Brienne.

Rory and Sergeant Mason spent time on their unicorns. While the stable hands took quality care of the animals, it wasn't the same as when the owners brushed them down and continued to strengthen the bond between steed and rider.

Derian only slept four hours but was in a wonderful mood, found his father and the two of them met the builders who were going to design their home, as well as Dr. Stein's lab.

"Come in," Lucien said.

Lucien's door opened and Master Jerron entered with two steaming mugs on a tray.

"Master Jerron, what a nice surprise, to what do I owe the pleasure?" Lucien asked.

Master Jerron set down the tray on the table, handed Lucien a mug, took one himself, and sat down in the chair across from Lucien.

"I came to share a cup of tea and to talk with you. Please, I made it myself," Master Jerron said as he motioned for Lucien to drink.

Lucien took a sip, then a bigger one.

"That was delicious," Lucien said.

"It's my own blend," Master Jerron said.

"What did you want to talk about Master Jerron?" Lucien asked.

"I wanted to see how you were doing. You have been through a lot young man," Master Jerron said.

"Thank you Master Jerron. Well, all in all I've….." Lucien suddenly found himself drained of energy. He could barely sit up straight in the chair.

"What's that my boy?" Master Jerron asked.

"I said….." Lucien found himself sliding out of the chair onto his knees on the floor. His vision was fading, and one thought screamed in his mind, "THE TEA!" He looked toward Master Jerron and said, "Why?"

Master Jerron stood from his chair, looked down and said, "All this fuss over a boy. Don't fight it. It will all be over soon."

Lucien did fight it though. He fought with all he had but he was losing strength fast. At that moment a new voice entered the room.

"Lucien, Master Stein and I were wondering….."

The voice cut short and suddenly Lucien was looking at two Master Jerron's. They instantly started speaking the language of magic and moving their hands. Lucien wanted to help but he was fading fast. With all the strength he could call upon he drew the knife he had on his belt and as he was falling he drove the blade into the foot of the false Master

Jerron. He heard him scream, there was a flash of light, then nothing.

Chapter Thirteen

Lucien awoke to Master Jerron standing over him. He immediately took up a fighting stance.

"Easy, Lucien, it's me," Master Jerron said.

"How do I know!" Lucien exclaimed.

"Lucien it's him," Arissa said as she came over and hugged him tightly.

"What happened?" Lucien asked.

"It was Malachi. Rob, Tom, and I confirmed it as he was taken away," Arissa said.

"Apparently this man entered the Great Wood unseen and without smell. Then mimicked my form and smell and then he gained access to your room and poisoned you Lucien. There was wolfsbane in the tea to weaken you and longsleep poppy to kill you. He didn't know you were immune to wolfsbane, so your natural healing ability fought the poison. I gave you a counteragent to bring you around faster. He was even able to mask the smell and taste of the wolfsbane from you. This man's magical skill at hiding and deception is unlike anything I've ever seen," Master Jerron said.

"Where is he now?" Lucien asked.

"He is awaiting questioning. We were waiting for you to awake before we began. If you are ready the others are waiting," Master Jerron said.

"I'm ready," Lucien said. A fury built quickly in him as he strode for the door.

"Your friends are waiting downstairs. I assured them you would be fine," Master Jerron said.

Master Jerron, Lucien, and Arissa went downstairs where Brienne, the twins, and Derian awaited. Brienne was the first to reach him with a hug.

"Will you ever stop worrying me cousin?" Brienne asked.

"No worries Brienne. I am alright," Lucien replied as he returned Brienne's embrace.

The twins were next. Both boys were smiling, but Lucien could smell the worry on them.

"We knew no cup of tea would be the end of you no matter what was in it," Rob said.

Lucien just smiled as the three young men embraced. When they were done Lucien found himself standing before Derian, who had a smile on his face, but like the others, the smell of worry hung about him.

"I was prepared to be very angry with you Lucien. I just got you into my life. I am not prepared to have you out of it anytime soon," Derian said as he leaned down and embraced Lucien awkwardly because of the height difference but no less heartfelt.

"Come Lucien, the king and the others are waiting for us," Master Jerron said.

Master Jerron led Lucien to a room where two guardsmen stood, one on each side of the door. When Master Jerron opened the door the scent of anger was heavy in the air, then as he entered the room, a flash of relief from those inside at seeing him alright, then back to anger.

There was a tinge of blood in the air coming from the man seated at the middle of the table. Lucien could see a large bandage wrapped the captor's foot. There was a spot of blood showing at the top of the bandage. The man also had manacles on his wrists that were carved with strange runes and pulsed a purple color. Lucien assumed these prevented Malachi from using his magic.

To the man's credit he didn't smell of fear only….resolve. Benagar stood behind him. At one end of the table sat his aunt and uncle. Timber stood behind them. His uncle was stone-faced, but fury came off him in waves. His aunt met his eyes and mouthed the words *Are you alright?* Lucien smiled and nodded. His cousins William and Quinn sat next to the king and queen. Lucien took the seat next to Quinn which was directly across from Malachi.

Master Jerron sat next to Master Stein, a testament to how quickly his genius and wisdom was respected, that he was allowed to attend this very sensitive closed meeting.

Lucien locked eyes with Malachi. The smell of anger came from the mage. Lucien could only assume it was anger at him for not being dead. Lucien smiled at him, and the mage's anger grew.

"Now that we are all here, let us begin. Malachi start from the beginning. Tell us why you are here. I do hope you won't be… difficult," Master Jerron stated.

"MASTER Malachi," he replied

"What?" Master Jerron asked.

"MASTER Malachi. I earned that title, same as you, dog-mage!" Malachi spat out.

At that instant the anger in the room became almost overwhelming. Being called a dog is the worst insult imaginable to a werewolf. Lucien wondered if Malachi was a fool or if he felt he had nothing to lose now that he was captured, or if he simply did not fear death.

Master Jerron simply sighed and said, "Difficult it is then. We want to know what the vampires have planned and why they are so determined to kill Lucien."

"And what do you offer me in return?" Malachi asked.

"Offer?" the king spoke and started to rise from his seat.

"Offer? You want an offer? Here is my offer. You tell us everything we want to know, and I won't leap over this table and tear your throat out!"

A slight nod from the king and Benagar grabbed Malachi by the hair and yanked his head back exposing his throat.

"My offer is this, you tell us what we want to know, and you won't live out the rest of your days in agonizing pain screaming for death!'

The king's claws and fangs were starting to extend, and his claws were beginning to score the table as his rage grew.

"You speak of offers when you have direct responsibility for the death of my brother, his wife, and 47 citizens of the Great Wood! You speak of offers when you snuck into my home. MY HOME! You attempt to murder my nephew with poison, a coward's weapon! Say *offer* again and you will have MY OFFER!" the king shouted in fury.

All in the room knew that Malachi's life hung by the thinnest of threads. Still no fear came from Malachi. If anything, he seemed more resolved

The queen slowly stood. She lightly touched the king's arm and said, "Killian we need to know what this man knows."

The king's fury lessened, and he retracted his fangs and claws. He nodded at Benagar who released the mage's hair. The king and queen sat back down.

"Do you have any idea how to make this man tell us what we want to know, because it seems he has no fear of death or pain," the king said.

"I believe I have an idea, if you all will indulge me," Master Jerron said.

The king nodded for him to go on.

"For those who can use magic there is no greater joy or pleasure. For some it becomes an obsession and all that they live for. I believe *Master* Malachi is one such person. So, for a man who lives only to use magic, what could the vampires offer him for his service? After all he can use magic anywhere for anyone," Master Jerron asked.

"Immortality," Master Stein replied.

"Yes immortality. I imagine the prospect of using magic for an eternity would be irresistible to a man like this. As we have seen death and pain hold no fear for him, but there is one thing all magic users fear. The Necros Dominae," Master Jerron said.

As soon as the words were spoken the smell of fear came from Malachi immediately.

"What is this you speak of that the very words inspire fear in this man?" the king asked.

"Roughly translated it means magic death. It is a ritual of punishment reserved only for the most heinous of magic using criminals. I think we can all agree this man qualifies for this punishment. His crimes are irrefutable," Master Jerron said.

"You cannot," Malachi said.

"Oh yes I can! *Master* Malachi and I will if you do not tell us what we wish to know!" Master Jerron shouted.

"What does this ritual do?" Lucien asked.

"Imagine a large part of your soul ripped away. Imagine an itch you can never scratch, a hole inside you that can never be filled. I only know of four that have had this spell placed upon them. Every one of them have gone mad. All but one took their own lives. The other sits in a room staring out a window every single day," Master Jerron said.

"But a deal of some sort must be struck, some incentive to help you. Death or imprisonment for life with these shackles on is still the end of magic for me," Malachi said.

"Unfortunately, sire he is correct and although it sickens me to my core there is only one deal I fear can be struck. After he tells us everything we want and only after the vampires are thwarted he will be banished from Arborreah never to return. He will go beyond the mountains in whatever direction he wishes to make whatever life he can. He will be marked magically so that if he does return I will be alerted and then he can be hunted and killed as he deserves," Master Jerron said.

"So, he gets to live," the king said as he slowly shook his head.

"There is someone else here who deserves to be heard. Lucien, this man has wronged you as much or more than anyone here. What do you have to say about all this?" the king said.

Lucien stood. "Thank you uncle. It's true I want this man dead. His crimes have earned him a slow, painful death. But after one thousand years the vampires are stirring and whatever they have planned will not be good for ALL the people of Arborreah. Stopping them is bigger and more important than my wants. We need to know what he knows and unfortunately Master Jerron is right. I see no other way to get him to speak than with this offer," Lucien said and then sat back down.

"I suggest you accept this offer. You won't get a better one," Master Jerron said.

"Very well, I accept your offer," Malachi said.

"What are the vampires planning, and why do they want Lucien dead so badly?" Master Jerron asked.

"The skygem has been found and they plan to finish what was started one thousand years ago. The covering of all of Arborreah in darkness," Malachi said.

"Impossible! The skygem was destroyed when Lucien Silverwolf struck it with his axe," the king exclaimed.

"The theory that the vampire mage Zorja and I have come up with is this; the skygem's power is great, but it is also wild, unpredictable, and almost delicate. Even Elymas, considered the greatest vampire mage to ever live respected its power. Using its power was a dangerous and precise thing which is why a mere axe strike was enough to catastrophically disrupt the magic being used that day. We believe there was an implosion before the outward release of power that swept over the battlefield, where the rebellion was being fought. We surmise the implosion was a way for the skygem to protect itself from absolute destruction. The skygem and the remains of Elymas' lab was discovered deep underground as the vampire's mining operation came across it in their digging, quite by accident. Among the books and writings that were found, there was a prophecy. The gist of it was that a human/wolf half-breed would stop the vampire's plans for an everlasting night. Once Gregor, the ruling Dracúl was told of this prophecy, he had his spy network be on alert for any news of such an unusual birth. Lo and behold one of his spies found out about Lucien. The Dracúl marked you for death, and no I do not know who or how the knowledge of your existence was discovered. When the 100 Blades failed he sent me," Malachi said.

There was silence when Malachi finished speaking as everyone absorbed what they had just heard.

The king stood, "Prince Rory."

"Yes, King Killian," Rory replied.

"I am going to send a raven to your father to tell him we will be travelling to Terramilene for a council of war. Guards!" King Killian called.

The guards from outside came in, "Yes sire!" they said in unison.

"Take the prisoner back to his cell," the king said.

"Yes sire!" the guards said.

They grabbed Malachi roughly, not caring in the least about his injured foot. When he was gone from the room the king continued.

"We will leave tomorrow for Terramilene. Timber, go find General Ravenseye. He'll probably be fishing at the lake. Tell him his king needs him to come out of retirement. Brief him on the situation and tell him to prepare to leave for Terramilene tomorrow," the king said.

"Yes sire," Timber replied and then left for the lake.

"Benagar. Spread the word to the pack leaders. Tell them to open the armories of ash and begin arming our warriors. They must do this quickly and the army must be ready to leave at a moment's notice," King Killian said.

"Lucien, please inform your friends as I'm sure they will be coming with us," the king said.

"I will uncle," Lucien replied.

"I suggest everyone get some rest, we leave for Terramilene at dawn tomorrow," the king said.

Everyone left the room after the king and queen. William went with his parents while masters Jerron and Stein went off together deep in conversation. Lucien, Quinn, Rory, and Sergeant Mason went over to the waiting area where their friends were standing, concern on their faces.

"My friends, please sit," Lucien said.

He shared everything that was discussed in the meeting. When he was done a heaviness seemed to descend upon everyone. The lightheartedness of the twins was gone, replaced by a seriousness and a stern thoughtfulness not usually a part of their demeanor. Quinn sat in silent thought.

"Well, it's getting late my friends. I suggest we heed the king's advice and try to get some rest. He wishes to leave at dawn for Terramilene. Good night," Rory said as he and Sergeant Mason turned to retire for the night.

The rest of the group stood and wished each other good night and then went to their rooms. Lucien and Arissa got undressed, turned down the bedside lamp, and got into bed. They were holding each other close, face to face.

"Do you think it may come to actual war?" Arissa asked.

"We'll know more after we meet with Rory's father, but yes I think it is likely," Lucien replied.

The two held each other tight before falling asleep.

Chapter Fourteen

The courtyard was a bustling ball of energy. It was filled with many people coming and going to ensure all was set for the journey to Terramilene, and possibly a longer trek after that. When Lucien and the other members of the group arrived, their wagon, outside of personal articles, was fully stocked and ready to go. Sunrise came and the last piece of the logistical puzzle was getting individuals into seats and moving toward the human city.

As Lucien was securing his items into the wagon his uncle, and another man, arrived at his side.

"Lucien, allow me to introduce General Kal Ravenseye," the king said.

The man had some grey in his neatly clipped hair and beard. He was of average height and had a slender build. He had piercing blue eyes that seemed to take in everything. While he had on clothes for the road, they seemed immaculately clean as if they were brand new.

"General it is an honor to meet you. My father spoke of you with great respect," Lucien said.

"I am sorry to hear of what happened to your family and village Lucien. I was very fond of your father. Since my retirement I sometimes take long excursions to the farthest reaches of the Great Wood. A bit of explorer in me I guess. That is where I was when you and your friends first came to the Great Wood. You were gone by the time I returned. I'm honored to meet you all, even under these circumstances," the general said.

Lucien turned to the group of friends who had walked up to meet the new individual and said to them, "Everyone, meet General Ravenseye. General Ravenseye is one of the few werewolves to graduate from the Citadel of the Martial. He kept going back to further his studies. His area of expertise is military tactics. He wrote many books on the subject. Many of his tactics and insights are used to teach others to this day."

"Heh, you are very kind Lucien. All I did was write a few books, but you and your friends, now there's something. All of you accomplished what no one else could, including me. You found and destroyed the 100 Blades. You killed Kane. If what the king says is happening with the vampires is true, I'm afraid we will need all of you heroes again. It is a pleasure to have met each of you. I look forward to learning more about all of you as we are on our journey. For now, please excuse me. It looks like we are getting ready to move out," the general said as he went to rejoin the king in loading up their own wagon.

As soon as the general turned to leave Rob and Tom did as well. Priya and Mara were all but jumping out of their skin in a poor attempt at waiting to say goodbye. When the girls left, Arissa spoke up, "Alright you two out with it. What is going on with you and the girls?"

Rob and Tom looked at each other, some color rose to their faces.

"We enjoy each other's company. We care about each other, but we have made it clear that we will be going home when this is all over," Rob began.

"They have also made it clear this is just a fling. They have no wish to leave the Great Wood," Tom said.

"We're all on the same page. Trust us Arissa, even though things with Priya and Mara aren't going anywhere, we all know what's going on, we would never disrespect them," Tom said a little too quickly.

Arissa hugged them and said, "Just making sure little brothers."

"Little brothers?" the boys answered.

Lucien chuckled as he climbed onto the bench of the wagon. He took hold of the reins to ensure all were set and locked into the correct positions. While going through the process he noticed Brienne talking to Rory. They were laughing at something and the way they looked at each other, Lucien knew that something was growing fast between them, and he couldn't be happier.

A quick trumpet like sound was made and though Lucien had never heard it before he instantly understood it was a signal for everyone to mount up and begin the procession. Brienne dropped her head in disappointment at the sound, but Rory placed his hand under her chin, raised her face to his and gave her a simple kiss on the cheek. When she turned to join the wagon carrying her family, General Ravenseye, Timber and Benagar, her face was flushed red and a wide smile overtook her face.

Rory then mounted Brownie, Sergeant Mason mounted his unicorn, named Stone, and they both rode up next to the royal family wagon. This would be the way they would depart the city. A strong, unified, force, riding off together to face whatever dangers await them.

The wagon carrying Malachi followed the royal family. A clean bandage was on the prisoner's foot, even though no one in the group of Lucien's circle believed he deserved to be tended to so well. He was not mistreated more than some rough handling while being transported from interrogation room, to holding cell, to cage. The cage, only big enough for the prisoner to sit in, had the cuffs kept around the wrists so he would not be able to perform any magic during their journey. If he had to use the bathroom, he would do so with the indignity of someone watching him. When he had to eat, he would need to figure out how with both hands cuffed. He sat in the back of the wagon while Master Jerron, Master Stein, and Lady Lucretia sat together on the driver's seat, all three talking amongst themselves.

Lucien's wagon was next. Arissa sat next to him while Quinn rode on the bench behind them. He was more than happy to give big smiles and waves to all those who came to watch them depart. While Quinn enjoyed the departure, Lucien kept his eyes locked on the mage who attempted to kill him. He wasn't officially tasked to keep an eye on the prisoner, but Lucien had no problem staring daggers into the caged man. Lucien had to calm his mind, as he was all but hoping Malachi would attempt something nefarious. Deal or no deal, there was a part of Lucien that wanted to end the breathing of that treacherous magic maker.

The twins and Derian were in the wagon big enough to carry the giant. When Tom gave the horses the call to go there was a long pause before the wheels started churning forward. It was a good thing their wagon was given two extra horses. They would be stressed to the limit with the weight they were pulling.

As the procession made its way out of the city, Lucien slowed his wagon some, allowing the twins to pull up next to his. He called over and asked, "Derian, do you have any idea what your father, Master Jerron, and now Lady Lucretia are up to? They've been practically inseparable and are always in deep conversation."

"I asked him. All he said was that what they were working on was too important to reveal until proven to work. I know he's excited by whatever they are working on. I'm just as curious as everyone," Derian replied.

The trip through the Great Wood was uneventful. Some of the malaise that had fallen over the group had lifted as the hours passed. Laughter found the young group again. That first night's camp there was good conversation. One was between King Farrunner and Arissa.

Arissa made her way to the fire where the royal family and a few others were finishing their meals. She asked, "King Killian, may I ask you a question?"

"Of course, my dear. What is it?" the king replied.

"Who rules the Great Wood when the royal family is away?"

"A fine question. Well, the title is Castellan, and at present that is Wes Morninglight. Probably the oldest living werewolf today. He served my father as advisor. When I told him he would be needed again, he practically leapt from his chair and begged to come along. To be a part of any fight against the vampires is a big deal. I told that old wolf that the vampires should count themselves lucky he wouldn't be there. I reminded him of his duty, and he grumpily nodded in acceptance, though even as I departed he still attempted to sway my decision. That old wolf's fangs are as sharp as his mind. Does that answer your question Arissa?" the king asked.

"Yes. Thank you," Arissa replied.

"Speaking of old Wes Morninglight. Did he ever tell you about the time him, your father, my father went to Terramilene and had a drinking contest against the entire inn?" Timber asked.

A smile began to creep over King Farrunner's face, but he quickly brought it back after recalling some of the details of that night and replied, "That's not a story for mixed company old friend."

"What? I.. I'm not going to be offended. What's the story?" Arissa asked, looking at Timber for help to convince the king to approve the telling of the story.

"Maybe another time, but not tonight," The king replied.

"Maybe another time," Timber said in agreement. He made eye contact with Arissa and gave her a wink and she knew that the time wouldn't be too long before she heard the story.

***

The group arrived at the southern gate of Terramilene to no fanfare, as King Farrunner requested in his raven-sent message to King Cromwell. He wanted to get to the palace as soon as possible and knew if the crowds were on, and in, the streets, it would slow things considerably. The matters at hand could wait no longer.

As the procession traveled through the city it was to be expected that some citizens would recognize them. Those citizens who did would wave and shout well wishes to those in the wagons, but all in all their progress was unhindered. They arrived at Castle Brightstone, where waiting attendants led the unicorn and horse teams away while soldiers took the wagon containing Malachi down to the dungeons. There were very strict guidelines given on how to handle the prisoner.

King and Queen Cromwell, along with Master Mattias, and another man were already in seats and waiting for the neighbors, allies and friends in the grand hall when the group entered. The stranger was in his early 50's, but still strong and well built. He stood straight and his uniform said he was someone important in the military. Like General Ravenseye, he had grey in his neatly clipped hair and beard. King Cromwell introduced him as General Whitmore Krain, commander of the armies of Terramilene.

"There are basins of water and washcloths in the councilroom. Please take time to wash off the dust from your hands and faces. When finished please find a seat as there is food and wine being prepared. I know we all wish to begin this council right away. Come," King Cromwell said as he led those attending the council to a large doorway flanked by two hulking guards. The guards opened the doors and then closed them again when everyone had passed through them.

"Come everyone, we'll wait by the fireplace until they're done," Queen Gwendolyn said.

Queen Sera, Brienne, Lady Lucretia, Rob, Tom, and Derian followed the queen to a waiting area where food and wine awaited them as well.

"I hope none of you feel left out. There are just certain protocols to follow as far as war councils go, and we'll be told the decisions made when they are finished," the queen said.

"We don't feel left out your majesty. The same protocols were followed in the Great Wood," Arissa replied.

"Good. Then come refresh yourselves. We will sit and talk. This will give me a chance to get to know you all a little better," Queen Gwendolyn said with a smile.

Inside the council room King Cromwell sat at the head of a long table with two guards standing behind him who looked even bigger than the guards outside the doors. On his right was King Killian, with Timber and Benagar standing behind him, then Willam and Quinn, then Lucien, then General Ravenseye, and then Master Jerron and Master Stein. On King Cromwell's left sat Rory with Sergeant Mason standing behind him, General Krain, then Master Mattias. When all were seated King Cromwell stood.

"This war council called by King Farrunner is ready to begin. King Farrunner if you are ready to tell us what you've learned, the room is yours," King Cromwell said.

King Farrunner stood as King Cromwell sat down and proceeded to tell the room what the vampires were planning, and about the prophecy concerning Lucien. He also told them his proposed plan of a small strike force going to destroy the skygem, while the armies of Terramilene and the Great Wood provide distraction by engaging the vampire army on the battlefield. When King Farrunner sat down there was silence while King Cromwell, General Krain, and Master Mattias processed what they had just heard. After a few moments King Cromwell spoke.

"This is dire news but it is obvious the vampires must be stopped and quickly. I believe King Farrunner's plan is a good one. Generals do you agree?" the king asked.

Both generals nodded. The king continued.

"Alright let's see if we can solidify this strategy. The floor is now open for questions and suggestions," King Cromwell said.

Master Jerron stood and began, "As far as the strike team to destroy the skygem, we need the mage Malachi. His ability to hide and conceal is like none I've ever seen, but he cannot be trusted. Master Mattias and I must go with the strike team to watch the mage closely, while he is leading us to the skygem. Lucien must also go. If there is any truth to this prophecy, it names him specifically as the one who will stop the vampires. Lucien you will select a few others to go, two more at most. Malachi told us the fewer people he has to conceal the easier it will be for him to hide the team and the better the illusion will be. Master Mattias and I will engage the vampire mage in battle while the rest of the team gets Lucien to the skygem so he can destroy it. Malachi claims there won't be many guards, if any. The vampire mage Zorja doesn't trust anyone to be near his work and he brooks no disturbances."

General Ravenseye stood and spoke next, "The vampires are ancient. They are faster and stronger, but for a thousand years our nations have prepared for this day. We've made ourselves strong. Our armies are well trained and both nations have vast armories of wooden weapons. Weapons that have been magicked and will punch through armor as if they were steel. They will not be facing slaves or humans who have been weakened by bloodletting. They will be facing two mighty armies and we will triumph."

General Krain stood and spoke next, "Fine words, fine words indeed general. We've known for some time that the vampires have a spy network, one we've never been able to uproot. We must assume they know something of our armies and tactics and strategies. What we need is someone who has been to the Nightlands. Someone who may have insights into the vampires' thoughts, or any kind of military knowledge at all."

There was a pause when the general finished speaking and sat down.

"There may be someone who has the knowledge we need," Lucien said.

"Who Lucien," King Cromwell asked.

Chapter Fifteen

Two palace guards brought in a man who wore prison garb. He was unshaven and had manacles on his wrists and ankles. The man's movement had an undignified manner, but even through that, he wore a smile on his face and had a cocky look in his eye as if he was an invited guest to a fancy dinner. He acted as if he wasn't a week away from being hanged. The guards forcefully sat Jackson Royce into an empty seat at the table. He folded his hands in front of him and looked over everyone else in the room. He nodded at Lucien and then just sat there waiting for someone to speak.

King Cromwell began, "Prisoner you have been brought here because it seems you may have information that we need."

"Ah, I see your majesty. And what information is that?" Jackson Royce asked as he leaned back with a look of comfort.

"Military information about the vampire kingdom. Numbers, strengths, weaknesses and any other insights that might be useful in battle against them," King Cromwell replied.

"I do have such information your majesty. In fact, I know it better than all but three or four individuals. Forgive my bluntness but what do you offer in return for this information?" Royce asked.

"These men and their offers," King Farrunner said. He rubbed his forehead as if trying to get rid of a headache then continued through his frustration, "Your reputation is as big as Kane's was. Your hands are soaked with blood, including the blood of my brother, his wife, and forty-seven others."

"I understand you must feel angry and frustrated King Farrunner. I know this is probably no consolation, but I did not participate in the attack on your brother's village. My job was to watch over the mage while he performed his magic. Concealing so many at one time taxed his strength and concentration and I was ordered to protect him if the need arose. I was never more ashamed of my time with the 100 Blades than on that day," Royce said this last part almost quietly.

Lucien knew the man called The Cobra spoke the truth. He could smell it. He wasn't sure how to feel about it though. Lucien felt for his uncle who was obviously struggling with having to give these men their freedom and knowing he had no choice but to do so. When Lucien thought about Malachi, hate welled up inside him, but that wasn't so with Royce. It's not as if he liked the man but hate for him just wasn't there. Maybe what The Cobra just revealed about feeling shame had something to do with it, or maybe it was just Lucien's instincts. Whatever it was he didn't have time to think about it now. King Cromwell leaned over, and the two kings exchanged whispers. King Cromwell put his hand on King Farrunner's shoulder and gave a squeeze before he continued.

"Why don't you just tell us what you want," King Cromwell said.

Royce took a deep breath and said, "A full pardon for all past crimes. Put it in writing, signed and sealed by both your majesties."

Dead silence in the room. The two kings faces grew sterner. Finally, King Cromwell slowly leaned over to speak in a whisper again with King Farrunner. The two kings spoke briefly and then both turned their attention back to Royce.

"Guard," King Cromwell said.

"Yes sire," said one of the guards who brought Royce in and was standing behind him.

"Go find royal scribe Bivens and bring him here. Tell him to bring paper, quill, ink, and wax," the king said.

"Yes sire," the guard replied, turned, and left to find the royal scribe.

"While we wait for scribe Bivens to arrive, you will tell us everything you know. When you are done if we determine that your information is indeed helpful, you will have your pardon. When we defeat the vampires and stop what they have planned you will have your freedom as well. This deal is fair and frankly more than you deserve. What say you?" King Cromwell asked.

"I agree to those terms. Your majesties are most fair. To begin, with your two armies combined you outnumber their forces two, maybe three to one," Royce began.

"Well, that's a good start," General Krain interjected.

"If you were dealing with any other beings but vampires it would be a good start general. The vampires that are in the Nightlands are all at least one thousand years old. The older vampires become the stronger and more powerful they become each year they live. They have no cavalry, but they don't need one, they are their own cavalry. With their speed they can match the charge of any force, even the Legion, and in my opinion that clash would be about even. Their armor is well maintained, and they have more than enough silver weapons to arm themselves with and unfortunately, plenty of wolfsbane," Royce said.

With this last statement you could see the air go out of King Farrunner.

"If I may your majesties," Master Jerron spoke up.

"Please, Master Jerron," King Cromwell replied, and motioned for him to speak.

"Master Stein came to me with an idea on the first day we met. He said he wanted to give a gift to the nation of the Great Wood for being so good to him and his son. Master Stein, the Lady Lucretia, and I have worked on nothing else. With a combination of science, magic, and the Lady Lucretia's incredible knowledge of herblore, we believe we have found a way to negate the effects of wolfsbane for at least a full day's time," Master Jerron said excitedly.

Master Stein had a calm smile on his face.

"Truly?" King Farrunner stated,

"This has been tried before over the centuries to no avail. Why do you believe there will be success now?" King Farrunner asked.

"Frankly sire we never had Mast er Stein before. The man's genius astounds me. He took us down avenues we had never thought of," Master Jerron said.

"Master Stein?" King Farrunner motioned for him to speak.

"First of all, sire, Master Jerron and the Lady Lucretia contributed equally and secondly, yes I believe that all we need to do is test our theory. We will succeed," Master Stein said with conviction.

"Master Stein when you were here last you made a request of me. To tell the Citadel of the Mind that you were indeed alive and would be coming back to the citadel in the future. I have done as you requested. Your tenure is reinstated, and a fully stocked laboratory is awaiting you. I will have a royal guardsman escort you and Master Jerron. On your way out feel free to have the Lady Lucretia join you. Is there anything else you require?" King Cromwell asked.

"Just a volunteer your majesty," Master Stein replied.

"I will volunteer," Timber spoke up.

"Timber you need not," King Farrunner said.

"With all due respect your majesty, time is of the essence. This must be tested now, and if it works they must then find a way to make and distribute this antidote to our entire army. Am I correct masters?" Timber asked.

"You are correct Timber," Master Stein replied.

"Besides, it is my duty to protect you and the royal family from any harm. So, none of you can volunteer for this. At least not on my watch, and Benagar's complaining will simply distract the masters from their work, so he cannot volunteer either," Timber said.

"He's not wrong about that," Benagar said with a smile.

"Very well but don't ever forget that you are family too my friend. Will your testing on Timber put him in harm's way Master Jerron?" King Farrunner asked.

"No, your majesty. If it doesn't work he will feel the normal unpleasant effects of wolfsbane. His life is not at risk, I promise you," Master Jerron replied.

"Very well then leave for the citadel now and keep us apprised of the results of your tests," King Farrunner said.

The two masters, Timber, and one of the guards that brought in Jackson Royce, left for the Citadel of the Mind.

"That could be a game changer your majesties," General Ravenseye said.

"Indeed. Prisoner, continue," King Cromwell said, purposely reminding The Cobra of his current status.

"The vampires are arrogant. They believe all who are not vampire are beneath them. Arrogance can be exploited. They are also desperate," Royce said.

"What do you mean," General Krain asked.

"The vampires are dying out. Fading away. Over the centuries hundreds of vampires have simply walked into the sunlight," Royce said.

"Why?" the kings asked almost in unison.

"Quite simply, for the last one thousand years the vampires haven't been living, they've been merely existing. Nothing thrives in the Nightlands. Humans, animals, most plant life, without the sun. They've barely been able to keep their human slaves breeding. What animals and plants they keep, and grow are barely enough to keep the humans alive. They must ration what blood they take from their slaves. Their system of surviving is on a razor's edge of collapsing. They won't turn any humans into vampires, they simply can't spare the slaves, and there are no purebloods being born. From what I understand, for a child to be born of two pureblood vampires there has to be a blood ritual, and the blood used must be strong. The last attempt was the Dracúl's own son and that didn't go well. The Dracúl killed and used the blood of twenty slaves, and still his son was born…..insane. You can see it clearly in the boy's eyes," Royce said.

"Tell us about the Dracúl. What kind of leader is he?" General Ravenseye asked.

"Strong, intelligent, and he believes what he is doing is to save his people," Royce replied.

"Ah scribe Bivens, please sit down," King Cromwell said as the royal scribe was let into the room.

"Thank you your majesty. I am here to serve sire." The small, bookish man stated.

"Gentleman I believe we can all agree that prisoner Royce has held up his end of the bargain with the information he has provided. While we will continue to gather information, at this juncture I believe we can begin to fulfill our part of the agreement," King Cromwell began.

Everyone at the table nodded in agreement before the king continued, "Scribe Bivens please draw up a royal pardon for all past crimes for Jackson Royce. It will be signed by King Farrunner and myself and we will both affix our seals upon it."

"Yes sire," scribe Bivens said as he spread out some paper and prepared his quill and ink to begin to write.

"Prisoner Royce, this pardon and your freedom will be waiting for you when the outcome of the coming battle is determined, whatever the outcome is. Until then you will remain a prisoner here. You will have a clean cell, clean clothes, and good food. Other comforts will be provided as well. This will give you time to think of any other information you may think is useful after our meeting today," King Cromwell said.

Scribe Bivens finished writing and began gently blowing on the paper to dry the document. When he was finished he presented the paper to King Cromwell. The king looked the paper over and nodded in approval. He signed it and then gave the paper to King Farrunner who also read it and then signed it with clear disdain in his eyes. A lit candle and a piece of black wax was given to the kings. They both held the wax to the flames and waited for enough wax to build up on the paper next to their signatures. They then pressed their royal seals into the wax fully legitimizing the document. King Cromwell slid the paper over to The Cobra and said, "Does this meet with your approval Jackson Royce?"

"It does. Thank you your majesties," Royce replied.

"Very well then, guards take the prisoner back to his cell. Be it heard from my mouth. He is to be treated well and to have a clean cell, clean sheets and the same food as a guest would. If this is not fulfilled by the guardsmen they will report directly to me. Also, tell the jailer he is no longer to be hanged. Instructions will be sent on how he is to be treated from here on," King Cromwell said.

"Ah if I may indulge your majesties a few moments more, I have another offer to make," Royce said.

"I don't know what else you could be bargaining for or what more you have to bargain with," King Cromwell said with an amused laugh.

"Well, I suppose I need to direct this offer to you Lucien. How would you like to know who killed your grandparents?" The Cobra asked.

Chapter Sixteen

As everyone left the meeting room, Lucien found himself deep in thought. He and the kings agreed to The Cobra's terms of his second offer. He would provide the information he had, and they agreed to give him what he wanted, strange as his request may be. Jackson Royce would give the information to Lucien if he survived the coming battle. If Lucien did not return then The Cobra would share his information to King Cromwell.

The group walked toward the waiting area and the kings began to tell the group what was coming. Lucien put thoughts of Jackson Royce aside as he realized that he and his friends were going to war and needed to focus. He was proud to have such friends in his life, and afraid to lose any of them. What they were facing was so much larger than anything they had faced before.

"There is much to do. Rory you must prepare the Legion, General Krain, the rest of the army," King Cromwell said.

"Yes sire," General Krain replied.

"Yes father," Rory replied.

"Lucien assemble the rest of your team. William, Quinn, with me. I must send a raven to Castellan Morninglight and tell him to send the army," King Killian said.

"Yes uncle," Lucien said.

Lucien was left with Arissa, the twins, Derian, and Rory as everyone else left the lounge area. He looked at them and took a deep breath.

"I need two volunteers for my team. Our mission is to destroy the skygem," Lucien said.

"Well one of those spots is mine and I'll brook no arguments about it from anyone," Arissa said casting her stern eye on everyone, landing finally on Lucien himself.

Lucien knew better than to argue.

"Alright I need one more," Lucien said.

"I will go. You will need me Lucien. I may be one, but I have the strength of many," Derian said.

"Alright Derian. I guess that completes my team," Lucien said.

"Well, I guess we're in the army now brother," Tom said as he smiled at Rory.

"Alright then. Derian come with me, we're going to the armorer. We have to get to work right away to get you some armor. You four need to be fitted for good leather armor.," Rory said.

"Rory, the twins and I have been preparing letters. Mine to Ben and Martha in Everly, and them to their parents in Hollister. As soon as we write what's happening now, can you get them sent out?" Lucien asked.

"Of course. When you are done with them, get them to me and I'll have the royal messengers take them right away. What will you four be doing now?" Rory asked.

"Well, I thought we would pay a visit that is long overdue," Lucien said.

The four walked up to the doors of the Citadel of the Martial and stopped before going in. They smiled at the mostly wonderful memories of the year they spent here forming their bonds and learning about themselves. They walked in and began to walk to the front desk. The acolyte behind the desk saw them and his eyes went wide. He rushed from behind his desk to greet them.

"Uh we are graduates of the Citadel. We have our diplomas here…," Lucien started.

"Please there is no need for that, everyone here knows who you are. You are Lucien Farrunner. You defeated Kane in single combat. You are Arissa, and you two are the Hollis twins, Rob and Tom. You all along with Prince Rory, found and destroyed the 100 Blades. Your names are going to be engraved on the wall of heroes, the youngest ever to receive that honor. We are all very proud," the acolyte said.

The four were caught off guard by that news. To have your name engraved on the wall of heroes is one of the greatest honors anywhere. It never occurred to any of them that their actions would have resulted in the highest award the Citadel provides to its graduates.

"Uh, thank you. We have come to visit the masters," Lucien said.

"Of course, you all know your way around. I'm sure the masters will be very glad to see you," the acolyte said.

The four visited their weapons masters first. Masters Stone, Clay, and Sinclair, and yes all three were very happy to see their former students. All three masters even allowed their classes to be interrupted to let the twins perform the battle between Lucien and Kane, which all three masters then proceeded to use that fight to continue that day's lesson. They visited Master Kai Shen last, their master of hand-to-hand combat. They knocked at his office door, and they heard his call for entry a few seconds later. The four entered and the room was just as Lucien remembered, warm and inviting. Master Kai Shen came from around the table smiling.

He bowed and said, "To what do I owe the pleasure of a visit from some of my most famous students?"

The four returned the bow a little red in the face. They were still a little embarrassed by all the compliments and attention.

"Forgive us master this is the first time we have had the opportunity to come and visit. It has been very hectic since we graduated," Lucien said.

"Nothing to forgive. I understand. Please sit, I would hear everything," Master Kai Shen said.

Lucien began to tell Master Kai Shen everything that had happened since graduation. When he got to the fight with Kane, he turned it over to the twins who were well rehearsed in re-enacting this now famous battle. When they were done they bowed and sat down. Master Kai Shen returned the bow.

"Your forms have much improved boys, have you all kept up with practice?" the master asked.

"Yes master we practice together most mornings," Rob replied.

"Master forgive me I didn't use the strategy you wanted me to when fighting Kane. Something told me to fight him in the manner in which I did," Lucien said.

"Don't apologize Lucien. You won. The wolf in you served you well," the master replied.

"What do you mean?" Lucien asked.

"Every living thing has instincts. Some greater than others. A werewolf's instincts are powerful. Instinct is a natural thing, it is when thought and feeling blend perfectly to help make a decision and choose a path, and it is almost never wrong. That is the something that told you to fight Kane your way. You have lightened a burden on my soul Lucien. Thank you," Master Kai Shen said as he bowed to Lucien.

Lucien returned his master's bow.

"Prince Rory sends his regards as well master. He wanted to come but his duties as commander of the Legion prevented him from joining," Arissa said.

"I understand. The prince hasn't been commander long, and even though he played no small part in smashing the 100 Blades, I imagine he still has much to learn," the master said.

"I'm afraid it's more than that master," Lucien said.

Lucien then proceeded to tell Master Kai Shen what was now happening, preparing for the upcoming war with the vampires. When he was done Master Kai Shen sat back in his chair, a thoughtful expression on his face.

"This is troubling news. After all this time the vampires stir. Although our vows as masters of the citadels prevent us from taking part in any wars, I'm sure a council of the masters will be held to discuss this. Forgive me, but I must cut our time short," the master said.

"Master do you have any advice for us for fighting in the upcoming battle?" Lucien asked.

Master Kai Shen looked at them for a moment then said, "Watch each other's backs. Keep turning and moving. Open yourselves up to the flow of the battle, trust your instincts."

They exchanged bows and the four left the masters office and then the citadel. They all felt renewed after their visit as they headed back to Castle Brightstone. There was still much to do.

The next two days were full of activity for everyone. Lucien, the twins, and Arissa got fitted for their leather armor. Derian had to spend much of his time with the armorers as they worked non-stop to make armor in his size. Master Jerron, Master Stein and the Lady Lucretia's experiment with the wolfsbane worked to the joy of everyone. The three worked with the royal family on a plan to be able to disperse the antidote to the entirety of the werewolf army, which was now camped outside the city.

The day before the armies were to leave for the Nightlands, the Farrunner family, along with Arissa, the twins, and General Ravenseye, had dinner together in a private room. The Cromwells were having dinner together in another room. The two families wanted a little private time together before tomorrow came. Derian, the Masters, and Lady Lucretia were busy at the north gate coating the archway in a substance they created that would disperse the antidote to the werewolf army as they pass through the gate, otherwise they would be with the Farrunners as well. When dinner was over, and the table cleared a silence fell over the room that Prince William broke.

"Father the armies leave tomorrow, and I would have your blessing to go with them," the prince said leaving most at the table with stunned looks on their faces.

"Absolutely not, you are the future king. It is bad enough I let your brother go and it breaks our hearts when he and your cousin and these three here who your mother and I have come to love as if they were our own, you ask too much William," the king said.

"Father you were king, and you still put yourself in danger hunting criminals. The stories are well known and retold with respect," the prince replied.

"That was different. It wasn't war and those brigands weren't vampires. I was foolish to put myself at risk. Foolish and selfish," the king said.

"The people don't see it that way father. I've thought about this. I'm not asking to be placed in the front. Give me command of the rear guard. The upcoming battle will go down in history and someday when I am king, the people will remember," William said.

"Is that what this is about? Glory? You see your cousin and brother and other names being shouted in the streets and songs being sung about them, and you also wish to have your name sung?" the king asked.

"No father, I do not envy them. They set an example. They inspire. Does it bother me to be left behind? Of course it does and not because I want a bit of glory for myself, but because I can help, because it is right," the prince said.

"What say you on this matter General?" the king asked.

The general put his wine glass down and said, "This is probably not the answer you wish to hear my king, my queen, but the prince is more than capable of commanding the rear guard. When he studied and attended classes with me he excelled in planning and battle tactics. He is far better at it than Prince Quinn, and if we're being completely honest, he may be better at these things than you my king."

"You've been quiet Brienne. Please say what you will," the king said.

The princess took a deep breath and spoke, "I have never been more proud of my brother than I am right now, or more terrified for him and for all who are going. William believes in doing what is right. He always has even when we were little. Although it will break my heart if he leaves tomorrow, I don't see how making him stay behind will help him become the wolf or the king he wants to be, he needs to be, or who we need him to be as a future king."

"Sera you have always been my rock. What would you have me do? Lock them all in the dungeons until the battle is over? Please tell me," The king pled.

The queen stroked the king's face and said, "Killian we cannot lock them away from the dangers of the world. We can only protect them for so long before they become young men and women and must face the world on their own. We hoped this day would never come. War with our ancient enemies no less. But many parents' hearts will be breaking tomorrow. Many parents will be worrying and waiting, and they will lean on each other for comfort. Are we to change our ways now and put ourselves above everyone else simply because of who we are? You are king and as always you will make the right decision."

With a heavy sigh the king said, "Timber, Benagar."

"Yes my king," the two answered in unison.

"I know I have asked much of you lately but will the two of you go and protect my sons as best you can?" the king said.

"You never ask too much of us. The king commands and it is our honor to obey," Benagar replied.

"Quinn you will ride with your brother," the king said.

Quinn answered his father, but looked at his older brother, "I will father. It will be my honor."

"Then it is settled, General Ravenseye," the king said.

"Yes sire,"

"My son will be taking command of the rear guard," the king said.

"Yes sire," the General replied.

"I suggest you all get some sleep. Preparations begin at dawn," the king said.

The king, queen, and General Ravenseye left the room, while everyone else came and embraced William, after which they took the king's advice and turned in for the evening. It would be their last night of comfort before the long road ahead.

Chapter Seventeen

The next day, just before dawn, final preparations were made for the armies to depart Terramilene. Tearful goodbyes were made throughout the city. The royal families were no exception. The Cromwell's and Farrunner's composed themselves and then stood on the steps of Castle Brightstone to wave goodbye to the passing armies and to show the people that they were with them. Lucien and his friends were behind the Great Wood army with the supply and medical wagons. Master Stein was in command of the medical wagons. He took the three top medical students the Citadel of the Mind had as his personal team. Lucien, Arissa, and Quinn drove one supply wagon. Quinn chose to ride with them because he wanted his brother to have his moment to shine all for himself. Derian and the twins drove another wagon. Derian was wearing his new gleaming armor, and new heavy boots. He declined a helm citing it impaired his vision. Arissa told him how handsome he looked, and you could see the blush even with his dark hued skin.

Prince Rory led the Hammeraxe Legion through the north gate first to the shouts of *Cromwell* from the crowds that had gathered to see the armies off. He waved to the people and the royal families watching from the castle steps. Queen Sera leaned over to her daughter and said, "Hmm that scarf on Prince Rory's arm looks familiar."

The princess returned her mother's knowing smile with a shy smile of her own.

"Brienne we will speak of this with the Cromwell's while we wait for everyone's safe return. I want you to know your mother and I approve," King Farrunner said.

The princess stood on her toes, kissed her father's cheek, and said, "Thank you," knowing how far her father had come in changing his mind about old customs that he had clung tightly to for so long.

There were many such tokens tied around many arms including Sergeant Mason who had a scarf on his arm from a certain herbalist. Behind the sergeant came the standard bearer carrying the flag of Terramilene; a black unicorn on a white field. To see the full might of the legion assembled, so many unicorns in one place moving in unison was a magnificent sight to behold. The regular army went next led by General Krain.

The Great Wood army was next. Prince William led them, riding a massive werewolf in third form. This was how the werewolf army presented itself while travelling through Terramilene. First form (human form) riding the third form wolves. Those riding as human form would change into second form once they went into battle. While the Great Wood army wore less armor and may not have shined as brightly as the Terramilene forces, they were impressive in their own way. To see that many werewolves in third form moving as one was a fearsome sight to see. Prince William looked every bit a prince of the realm, handsome and proud. He was flanked by Timber and Benagar. General Ravenseye came next. The standard bearer was behind them. Their flag bore a grey wolf on a field of green. The wolf army stopped just before the northern gate. Master Jerron and Master Mattias stood underneath the gates archway and began speaking the language of magic and making intricate hand gestures. The archway began to glow a purple-greenish color which interacted with the brightstone the archway was made of for a beautiful affect.

The mages magic activated a substance that was painted on the archway the night before. Every werewolf who passed through the gate was to have at least two waterskins. After passing through the gate each werewolf was to mark one waterskin in some way and then save that waterskin for just before they entered the Nightlands. They were all told multiple times that the wolfsbane immunity lasted for one day.

The two masters finished their spellcasting then got into a wagon with the Lady Lucretia as she waited with Malachi, who was caged and magically manacled in the back. Master Jerron already had his own waterskin prepared. The werewolf army then began to pass through the gates. Once through, they marked their waterskins as instructed.

Lucien and his friends were at the back, and even there they were recognized by the people and their individual names were called, thanking them and wishing them good fortune. They came in sight of the palace and waved goodbye to the royal families. The families waved back and a short ride later, they were through the gates. Quinn marked his waterskin and that was it, they were on their way north. On their way to battle an ancient and powerful enemy for the fate of all.

INTERLUDE

The Dracúl sat on his throne and thought about the fate of his people. He did this most days for hours on end. A servant came and told him that a raven had come with a message from one of his many spies. The Dracúl told the servant that yes, he would receive it now, inwardly thankful for the distraction. The servant went to the throne room doors, opened them, and told the soldier waiting outside that the Dracúl would see him now.

The soldier walked in stone faced. He walked with his shoulders back. His black armor gleamed. His very manner spoke the word pride. Seeing this soldier like this reassured Gregor that not all of his people had fallen into despair. That there were still many who took pride in who they were and believed that their Dracúl would repair their failing kingdom. The soldier stopped at the dais, dropped to one knee, and awaited his Dracúl to address him.

"Rise soldier," the Dracúl said.

The soldier rose and waited.

"You have a message for me?" the Dracúl asked.

"Yes Dracúl," the soldier replied and held out a small piece of paper.

One of the Dracúl's royal guard took the paper from the soldier and gave it to Gregor. Gregor unraveled the small piece of paper and a smile formed on his face. The message read: "The armies of the Great Wood and Terramilene will be leaving for the Nightlands in two days' time."

"What is your name soldier?" the Dracúl asked.

The younger vampire seemed to stand up straighter, honored that his Dracúl wanted to know his name.

"Dennon, Dracúl," the soldier replied.

"Dennon tell General Vameer to ready the army. We'll be having visitors in about a week," the Dracúl ordered.

"Yes Dracúl," the soldier replied with a smile on his face.

The Dracúl sat back in his throne also smiling. Finally, things were coming to a head. A coming battle was just what his people needed. Something to inspire them. Living breathing enemies to fight. His people had been battling despair for centuries and they were losing. But here was an enemy that they could defeat and defeat them they would. The Dracúl's smile widened, showing his fangs as he ran his fingers along the grip of his greatsword Reaper, and began thinking of the battle to come.

****

The days spent travelling to the Nightlands were used for drilling, going over plans, and practicing. The Hammeraxe Legion and the Great Wood army practiced charging together to maximize effectiveness and to make sure they filled gaps during the charge without getting in the way of each other. This is where the twins spent much of their time during the day, learning to charge. They were paired with two young wolves who were also brothers, Lupos and Lobos Swift. The eager young wolves were honored to be riding into battle with two of the heroes who destroyed the 100 Blades. The four worked together as if they had practiced together for years.

Derian spent his time between planning with Lucien and his team and drilling with Prince Rory and the Legion. He would mimic their forms as they practiced with their hammeraxes. Derian used his hammer and threw himself into the training of how to properly use and fight with his own heavy weapon.

Lucien, Arissa, the mages, and Derian would get together and go over the plan. Even though it was simple, they went over it every day, nonetheless. Malachi would make their wagon and them completely invisible in every way. They had to go slow to keep the illusion as perfect as possible. The terrain was flat which helped. The lab which had the skygem was three miles west of Castle Obsidian. It was a simple one-story building and the skygem was on the roof. They would start their slow journey at sunrise, the army would begin their journey an hour later. The hope was that the battle would begin just as they would arrive at the skygem. Malachi told them that travelling in the Nightlands was not what most people thought. When the sun was bright outside, being inside the Nightlands was like a regular day at its cloudiest, dark, but vision wasn't hindered. Only at night is it truly dark.

Dr. Stein spent his days telling his teams what he expected of them. The three young minds that were on his personal team were happy to be there and learn from Dr. Stein whose name had become legend in the halls of the citadel. Here before them was a human being who looked barely 40 but was actually closer to 300 years old.

The companions would gather for dinner after a long day of practicing and training, before turning in for the night exhausted.

Lucien was preparing his and Arissa's tent for their last night's sleep before entering the Nightlands the next day.

"Lucien can we talk?" Arissa asked.

"Of course," Lucien replied sensing the seriousness in her voice.

Arissa sat across from him and began.

"For the first part of my life I never felt any real fear. You just get used to the bad treatment and that's what you came to expect. As far as fear of death I just assumed that whatever came after had to be better than my life as it was. Then I was accepted to the citadel and all of a sudden I had a family, a real family one that loved me and that I loved. Then came you and I and what we have and for the first time I know real fear because now I have so much to lose. Tomorrow we all go into battle against the most powerful foes any of us have ever faced. Our family will be going to war so that we may accomplish our goal and I fear for them. I have also feared us and how I feel for you, and I know you feel for me. I feared giving you my heart for so many reasons that simply do not matter anymore. I will fear this no more. This may be our last night together and I would tell you Lucien Farrunner what is in my heart. I love you. I am sorry I made you wait to hear that. I am sorry I didn't trust what we have."

"There is nothing to be sorry for Arissa. I've known for awhile what is in your heart, and I would have waited as long as it took to hear those words. I love you too Arissa, with everything that I am," Lucien replied as he took her in his arms.

"Then love me Lucien. Love me," Arissa said.

They made love that night as only the young and in love can. They made love as if it may be their last night on this world. There was hunger and passion in it, and when they were finally finished, breathing heavy and exhausted there was no more *still friends* but only *I love you.*

Chapter Eighteen

The next morning a large group gathered at the western border on the edge of the Nightlands. Four strong plow horses attached to a large wagon waited. Master Jerron and Master Mattias were in the back with the magically manacled Malachi. Arissa, Lucien, and Derian were saying their goodbyes to the rest of the group.

"It feels strange for us to not be together, somehow not right," Rob said with Tom and Quinn nodding in agreement.

"We wish we were going with you cousin," Quinn said as strong goodbye hugs began.

"We wish you were coming as well, but we all have our parts to play. Quinn, watch over William, he needs your strength now," Lucien said while embracing his cousin.

"I'm just glad the three of you know how to get your armor on by yourselves," Prince Rory said jokingly.

Lucien and Arissa had their leather armor on and Derian had his custom armor on as well. For as little time as the smiths had to make it, they did an excellent job. Lucien and Arissa also had bandoliers of magically enhanced wooden stakes that would punch through armor as easily as steel. The smiles from the prince's little joke faded as the embraces and goodbyes continued. Arissa hugged the twins, Rory, and Quinn as she fought back the tears beginning to form in her eyes.

"Promise me we will all be together again when this is over," Arissa said.

"Arissa.....," Rory started.

"I don't care if you mean it, just say it," Arissa pleaded.

The boys looked at her and promised.

"Good," Arissa said looking relieved.

Master Stein was already at the wagon saying goodbye to the other Masters, when the group came over. He embraced his son and the others as they climbed into the wagon.

"Watch over each other. Protect each other, and stand true," Master Stein said with a straight back and a face full of composure. His act was one done well.

"One more thing Lucien, if you can, see if you can return these elders to us as well. Mine and Quinn's father would hate to be bothered with replacing them, even though they are, well, old," Prince Rory said, Quinn smiling next to him.

"I will remember that Prince Rory," Master Mattias replied.

"Are you sure?" Rory asked.

"And I don't know why you're smiling Prince Quinn, you know I'll remember," Master Jerron said.

"I look forward to you making me pay for laughing at Rory's fine jest," Quinn replied.

The two masters had matching bracelets which linked them to Malachi's manacles. The idea was that through this link they would be able to make sure that Malachi deviated not one iota from the task of hiding them. With a look from Master Jerron, Malachi began chanting words of magic. One minute the wagon and all in it were there, the next they were gone. There was no sound from them and even Quinn couldn't smell them. There was no sign of them moving, no tracks or dust wafting up from their passage.

The remaining group stood in place for a moment longer before returning to the main army. When they rejoined the main force, goodbyes were had again as Rory, the ever-present Sergeant Mason, and the twins went to the front. Prince Quinn joined his brother at the rear guard, and Master Stein went to take command of the medical tents.

When Rory reached the front lines he was joined by General Ravenseye. The general was riding a massive werewolf in third form. The general turned to face the army, he held up his marked waterskin, and drank it. Then Prince Rory handed a sprig of wolfsbane to the general that he then showed the army. The general took the wolfsbane, put it under his nose and inhaled deeply. The general felt that the wolf army should be left with no doubt that the antidote worked before the coming battle. The wolf army then followed the general's example and drank their own marked waterskins. The mass of werewolves were now completely confident in the antidotes effectiveness.

Two hours had passed since Lucien's team began their trek to the skygem lab. They should be a little over halfway there by now, which meant it was time for the main army to enter the Nightlands.

Passing from the bright sunshine into the gloom of the Nightlands was an odd sensation. The temperature drop was considerable. The terrain was barren. One could see the mountains to the sides and behind the city in the distance. The sky had the same dark haze as everywhere in this bleak land. Though difficult, it was possible to mark where the sun was in the sky, but a person could look directly at that spot with no squinting or discomfort. It was more than evident none of the sun's rays made it to the inhabitants of this land. It was shocking anything could live in this place.

Rory called for a halt when the army was about a half mile from the city's front gates. He and General Ravenseye and Sergeant Mason, who carried the flag of parlay, rode away from the army until they were about one hundred yards from the gates of the vampire city. Ten minutes after the portcullis rose and the giant doors opened. Three massive vampires in black armor walked toward them. The vampire in the middle had a huge greatsword strapped across his back. Even at this distance Rory could sense what could only be described as *age* coming off them. The two flanking vampire's pale faces were set in stone, the middle one had a look of annoyance on his face. The three stopped just before Rory and his two riding mates.

"So, this is what they send to treat with me. A young boy and an old dog," the Dracúl said.

A low growl came from the werewolf the general was riding. The general leaned down and put a hand on the werewolf's neck and the growling stopped.

"Well, boy, you have something you wish to say?" the Dracúl asked.

"You have committed crimes that you must answer for, vampire," Rory said practically spitting out the last word.

"Crimes? Crimes! Since when does the deer accuse the lion of crimes?! No, boy, I think not. Go. Go back to your army and wait for death, it will be coming soon enough," the Dracúl said, then turned and walked back through the city gates. Rory, Genera Ravenseye, and Sergeant Mason rode back to the army.

Rory wished the general good fortune as the general rode to the command pavilion where he and General Crain would receive messages from the battle itself and give orders accordingly. Rory and Sergeant Mason went to the front of the cavalry where they would wait to give the command to charge.

Shortly after Rory was set and in position he could see the vampire army swarm out of the city gates and take the field. He tried to remain calm, to hold his adrenaline in check, but when facing such a foe it is impossible not to feel something, including fear.

A horn sounded and the vampire army began to move forward, slowly gathering speed, but it did not take long before the vampire army quickly closed the distance.

Rory gave the order for the archers to begin firing. It was a distinct advantage as the vampire couldn't counter with arrow volleys of their own. No trees grew in the Nightlands so no arrows or bows could be made. A rider next to Rory sent a very long pole into the air with an arrow flag attached. It was the signal for the archers. They were expected to loose three salvos before the distance between the two charging armies closed to a distance where the chances of hitting your own men became too great. Hundreds of arrows would fly, making the dark sky almost black while slowing down the vampire charge as the arrows fell. Thirty seconds went by and not a single arrow flew. Rory turned in his saddle to see if he could see what was wrong. He couldn't see what was wrong, but he could hear the screams of the dying.

Chapter Nineteen

William and Quinn waited with the rear guard. They both knew how important the rear guard's role was to the coming battle. They were the last stand and must reinforce places in the battle that look like they might crumble. The rear guard must make sure the army doesn't get flanked, and they must act fast.

Growing up, William was a serious boy. He wasn't unhappy, he just smiled very little and seemed to have little fun. He and Quinn were opposite in demeanor, but there was love between them. In the quiet moments of their youth, William was always a rock. When Quinn would have difficulties as a kid, or into the teenage years, it was William he would confide in. Quinn knew, without it ever being said, his brother would keep the secret and do whatever needed to be done to be a protector. They didn't say it often, but they loved each other greatly.

Quinn never looked up to his brother more than he did right now. The Farrunner princes heard the enemy horn blow and knew it was only a matter of time before the battle began. They saw the flag for the archers go up. They saw the archers begin to jog to their positions where they would begin firing. Before a single arrow flew, the ground burst open between the archers and the rear guard. Hidden doors opened from the ground and vampires poured out like black ants . Archers wore light leather armor and were no match for vampires in full plate. In an instant the arrow attack was routed, and men died quickly.

"The vampires laid a trap Quinn! We have to help those men. If we don't stop them the army will be set on in front and behind!" William shouted.

Quinn changed into third form and William into second form. William leaped onto Quinn's back, howled, pointed his spear and led the rear guard into battle, knowing that if they did not triumph here and now, the battle would be lost before it's began.

****

Lucien and his group were a little over halfway to the skygem lab when they heard the first horns sound. No one said anything as they were all trying to keep as quiet as possible, but Lucien could feel the nervous tension rise. Arissa met his eyes, neither of them had to speak to know what the other felt, fear for their friends and family. Derian sat alone on the wagon's driver seat, but Lucien could see the unease form in his massive shoulders, and he could smell the fear come off of him. Lucien knew this fear Derian felt was not for himself. He and Arissa made their way to the front of the wagon silently, and each put a hand on one massive arm to let Derian know he was not alone. To remind him he would never be alone again. Derian looked at them both with a grateful smile.

They continued on for another hour until they the lab came into sight. A squat building, nothing fancy or worthy of note to indicate how important it was to the vampires. It was one floor and on the east side of the roof sat the skygem.

As they got closer to the building Lucien felt as if something was gently pushing him in the back. Lucien turned around to investigate but found nothing. He then felt as if someone was pulling him from behind. It was an invisible force and Lucien did not understand the meaning of it.

Master Jerron caught Lucien's eye and made a gesture that let Lucien know what was happening. Lucien removed the harness that held his swords, took one and slowly began to unsheathe it. He saw a white-blue glow coming from the blade. He remembered Master Jerron casting his randomizer spell on his swords. It seemed they had now revealed the purpose of that spell. To lead Lucien to his apparent destiny, destroying the skygem. He put the harness back on and saw Master Jerron give him a wink and a smile. Then there was an explosion of light and heat, then screaming, then burning flesh.

****

"My prince you must sound the charge. Something has happened to the archers; you must trust Prince William to take care of what is happening back there. The vampire charge is building if we do not match their charge with our own we will be overrun, and all will be lost!" Sergeant Mason shouted.

Rory knew he was right. He hated having to ignore those screams of dying men coming from the rear of the army. But that is part of being in command, hard decisions.

"Sergeant Mason sound the charge," Rory said.

Rory pulled Skullsplitter from it sheath on his saddle, raised it up for all to see and steadied himself. Like all, he awaited the signal to charge.

Sergeant Mason took his horn and blew. There was an immediate reaction as the Hammeraxe Legion raised their fabled weapons in the air to match that of Rory's. The wolf army raised their spears in the air a fraction of a second later. Prince Rory lowered Skullsplitter and the charge began.

The Legion led the charge with the wolf cavalry slightly behind. The idea was for the Legion to meet the initial charge, and the wolves to fill in any gaps. It didn't take long for the charge to get up to speed. Rory felt as if he were riding on thunder itself. War cries and howls went up from men and wolf alike adding to the sound of the charge.

The vampires were coming fast now, and it would only be seconds before impact. Rory took those last few moments to think about his family, friends and all the innocent people who would suffer if he failed. Then his training took over and he quieted his mind.

The vampire army was a mass of black armor, pale faces, and silver weapons. Three seconds until impact, two, one! The armies just seemed to crash into each other. Rory felt his entire body shake and then he was swinging, caving in chests, taking limbs, and yes splitting skulls. Though not killing blows to vampires they felt the pain of them and were incapacitated by them. The wolves followed up with their magically enhanced wooden weapons finishing any hurt vampire with killing blows. When killed the vampires just crumbled to dust leaving empty suits of armor. Rory felt impacts run up his arm as he delivered blows and absorbed blows to his shield and armor.

There were roars of battlerage, screams of the dying, and clashing steel. Brownie was bucking, kicking, biting, his horn dripped with blood.

Time began to have no meaning. Rory didn't tire. On the top of his chest, he felt the heat of the gem he received at graduation. He knew it was helping replenish his energy and stamina, but he didn't think it was made to last this long. He felt no pain, he just kept moving.

Turning with Brownie arm swinging, realizing he was adding his own war cries to the noise of battle. The smell of blood and foulness filled the air as men and wolves voided themselves as they died.

There was no way of knowing if they were winning or not. There seemed to be equal amounts empty armor as bodies littering the field. He realized he hadn't seen Sergeant Mason in awhile. He hoped that the battle had simply swept him in another direction. He didn't want to entertain the thought of him being gone. There seemed to be no shortage of enemies and Rory rode into a knot of them. He took two heads before they knew he was upon them. Rory was turning to find another vampire to kill when a long black blade erupted through Brownies neck and then the blade was torn free. Brownie screamed and fell already dying. Rory's training took over and he rolled free. He felt the pain in his heart and soul as his loyal friend, bonded to him since he was a child, died.

Standing before Rory was Brownie's killer, Dracúl Gregor. Rory was a large young man. Six foot four and 230 pounds of broad-shouldered muscle, but he felt small compared to the vampire lord.

"I told you death would find you on the field boy. Stand up, it seems we won't be interrupted," the Dracúl said.

He was correct, it was as if both armies sensed these two leaders were going to fight and the main battle just continued around the combatants. It was as if a space opened up for just the two of them.

"I think this has gone on long enough boy. Time to die," the Dracúl said.

Dracúl was on Rory in a burst of speed, swinging that huge black blade. It was all Rory could do to get his shield up and defend. The force behind the blows were the strongest Rory had ever felt. It wasn't long before the magic of his gem was exhausted, and he could now only rely on his training. The vampire lord was relentless, and Rory's shield began to bend, and his shield arm was going numb.

Rory tried to mount an attack, but the vampire had a counter for everything the prince tried. The vampire smirked and attacked again; raining blows down on Rory's shield arm. The shield bending and caving in around his arm which now screamed in pain. Every blow shook his entire body until Rory was down on one knee doing all he could to block one more blow as the realization set in that this was it. The vampire was toying with Rory, and when his fun was over, Rory was going to die. While the heavy blade continued to smash down on what was left of his shield, a sadness crept over Rory. He knew his loss would crush his family and friends. He thought of Brienne and what they had begun, ended far too soon. He felt he had failed but hoped he had done enough so that Lucien would succeed.

"Don't feel bad boy. You never stood a chance. I am simply your better," the Dracúl said.

Everything seemed to slow down for Rory as the Dracúl raised his sword above his head for the killing blow. Before it could be brought down Rob came spinning from seemingly out of nowhere and drove his spear through the back of the Dracúl's knee. The vampire screamed in pain. An instant later Tom came spinning from the other side driving his spear through the vampire's armpit and through his chest. The vampire lord's eyes went wide then clenched in rage. He dropped his sword. His body began to shake and a look of intense focus came over his face. The way Tom's spear was driven through the Dracúl's chest his heart should have been pierced and he should be dust. It was as though through sheer force of will he was holding himself together.

"Rory, you must get up and end this now. We can't hold him for long!" Rob shouted.

Rory stood, as if in a dream. His shield arm hung useless. He picked up Skullsplitter with his good right arm. He didn't remember it being this heavy.

The Dracúl looked up and said, "Slain by children," he was laughing as Rory mustered every iota of strength he had left, swung Skullsplitter, and took Gregor's head. He finally turned to dust. Rory then collapsed in a heap. The boys were on him in an instant.

"C'mon Rory stay with us," Rob said.

"Tom why is half your face painted?" Rory asked before slipping into unconsciousness.

That's when a strong wind from the northwest buffeted them all.

****

The archers were routed, none of them able to get off a single arrow. As Prince William rode into battle he noticed some things. William's force outnumbered the vampires who had come up through the ground at least two to one, but they were still emerging. Wolves in second and third forms communicate through a series of yips, howls, snarls, and growls. William ordered packs of about 100 wolves each to stem the tide of vampires coming out of the holes. He wanted the holes collapsed and then fires built on top of them. It wasn't long before the battlefield became a maze of smoke. The next thing William noticed was that the vampires who were already out, many had broken any semblance of discipline and were just standing there feeding on the archers. It was as if the smell of fresh, vital blood robbed them of any other thought but feed. It was an easy thing to stake them while they were in this state. William slew three vampires this way himself before the rest of the vampires regained their senses and mounted some sort of counter attack. Even though by then it was too late for these remaining vampires this was when the battle was at it's most dangerous.

This became a different type of enemy for the wolves as the vampires were faster and stronger after consuming the fresh blood. They were more dangerous in every regard. In the last wave, with considerably fewer vampires to fight, many more wolves died than the first wave where the numbers, and surprise was heavily on the vampires' side.

When that skirmish was finally over, William, still sitting atop Quinn, noticed his brother limping. William dismounted to ease his brother's discomfort. After a quick look at the cut in the rear right leg of Quinn, William told his younger sibling to get medical attention. Quinn wouldn't leave the field even when Timber and Benagar tried to command him to go to the medical tents. The two older warriors had many wounds of their own. To William they looked younger and more vital than he had ever seen them. It was as if battle had awoken a part of them that had been asleep. In the end they tended Quinn's wounded leg themselves and allowed him to stay but he could no longer carry William, or anyone else.

William did assign small packs to watch over the holes that raged with bonfires. The wounded who could return after receiving medical attention were ordered to continue to bring wood to keep the fires going strong. Every wolf set as a sentry at those openings all but hoped more vampires would arrive.

William reformed the lines of the rear guard, the real battle had already been underway for a while and as much as he wanted to charge in and help, he knew the responsibility of the rear guard. He must watch and then only commit troops where and when needed. So, he stood there with Quinn, Timber, and Benagar watching the battle closely, wondering about their friends. Watching and waiting.

****

The horses were burning. Screaming and burning. One moment they were riding along silently, the next there was a flash of light and heat, and the horses were engulfed in flames. The horses thrashing flipped the wagon and broke free, just to run off a few feet and die.

Derian, Lucien, Arissa, and Master Jerron landed agilely. Master Matthias and Malachi did not. Master Mattias hit his head and Master Jerron was tending to him, trying to get him to regain his senses while looking around at who, or what, caused the madness they were in. Malachi hit hard on his shoulders. The shackles prevented him from landing without injury. He was getting to his knees when a voice came from the roof of the lab.

"Malachi, you traitor! We offer you immortality and you betray us!" Zorja shouted.

"No Zorja! I had no choice please. Release me and I will help you end them," Malachi pleaded as he held up his shackles to the vampire mage.

"Help me? My Dracúl needed your help with his business outside the Nightlands, but I never needed your help. Goodbye Malachi," Zorja yelled.

He spoke magics words and made hand gestures and a bolt of blackness struck Malachi in the chest. Malachi let out a scream that pierced everyone who heard it. The blackness spread out from Malachi's chest and just seemed to devour him until nothing was left of the shackled mage, just empty manacles. Only then did the vampire turn his attention to the rest of the individuals. He looked down from the roof of the lab as if they were a minor annoyance.

"Kill them," he said.

The lab door burst open and vampire warriors came pouring out. Derian leaped out from behind the overturned wagon bellowing a war cry. The roar and the sheer size of the being before the vampires froze them momentarily. Faster than could be believed, Derian torqued his body hard, swung his hammer one-handed from left to right and took the first three vampires heads off their shoulders. Their armor collapsed in heaps of dust, black steel and silver weapons.

Lucien jumped out from behind Derian and headed straight for the skygem. He was met by two vampires. He drew his blades, which were still glowing blue-white and tugging slightly upward toward the corner of the roof where the skygem was and readied them for battle. Lucien called upon the power of the wolf, quieted his mind, and strode toward the warriors awaiting him. There was no fear, worry or apprehension, only the flame.

Arissa was firing from behind the wagon, each arrow finding a vampire heart. She was covering the two masters who were now engaging the vampire mage in battle. Her arrows found the mark on every one of the vampires, dropping them all but where they stood. When a moment of pause was found she would try to send one at the vampire mage Zorja but it was obvious he had some form of barrier of protection around him. Her arrows would simply disappear when they got close to him.

All but two, who were engaged with Lucien, of the twenty vampires that exited from the lab tried to bring down Derian. The outcome for most was the same. If their heads weren't completely torn off they were so injured they couldn't fight again. They would dart in and not withdraw fast enough and were smashed by Derian's hammer or fist. As a vampire lay there mangled, waiting to heal enough to get back in the fight, Arissa would stop shooting, rush in and stake them destroying them completely.

Lucien had a significant disadvantage in reach against the two vampires he was fighting. The two worked in concert, diving in and swiping their long blades at different angles, trying to throw the young warrior's balance off. When one got a little overextended Lucien parried the blade, dipped down just a little and caught the vampire directly in the throat. With a harsh downward movement, the blade opened up the vampire warrior from throat to stomach, Lucien took his head and then there was only one.

Back and forth the duo swung at the other but the lone vampire was getting sloppy, and Lucien could see three moves ahead what was going to happen. The vampire took a massive swing with his two-handed sword, arcing down at an angle that would have cut Lucien from neck to ribs if he wouldn't have used the vampire's momentum against him. Lucien deftly stepped into the vampire, putting his right shoulder into the mid-section of the pale face, ducked under the arms of his opponent and stepped out, swung quickly with one of his blades which sliced off both hands of the vampire. He then continued his own spin, stood up tall and swung his other blade straight across. This move removed the head of the remaining vampire in his way.

Lucien sheathed his blades, sprinted for the lab and leaped. He caught the edge of the roof and pulled himself up. There before him was the skygem. It wasn't activated but he could still feel it's power. He could feel his blades nudging him forward. The vampire mage was still engaged in battle with Masters Mattias and Jerron, and he didn't seem to know Lucien was there. Lucien withdrew his blades which no longer glowed now that he was where he was supposed to be. He saw the wound in the center of the skygem that his namesake caused so long ago. It was longer and looked deeper than he imagined. Lucien put his two swords together as close as possible and then drove both blades into the slot that Lucien Silverwolf's axe caused. The swords went deep enough to do what Lucien had in mind. He grabbed the two hilts and started to pull them away from each other. He hoped the magic in the blades that made them unbreakable held as he began to pull. He pulled hard and nothing happened. His swords held but so did the skygem. He took a breath and pulled again, straining, sweat began to pour down his face. He felt muscles pulling in his back and shoulders.

"So, finally, the *half-breed*." The vampire mage said.

Lucien turned to see the vampire mage looking at him with a mixture of anger and annoyance. Lucien looked down to see both masters on the ground not moving, Arissa running to check on them. Derian was still fighting, and smashing, multiple foes.

"We sent Kane and the 100 Blades. We sent that fool Malachi, and still, you wouldn't die. I must admit for a moment I started to believe that prophecy I found. I wonder if no one found it and read it, would you be here right now? No matter our fates are not dictated by words on a paper from unknown authors. Our fates are our own! We decide! It seems you were fated to die here far from home. Goodbye half-breed," Zorja said.

The master vampire mage started to speak the language of magic and raise his hands, when suddenly his hands went to his throat as an arrow protruded from it. The mage made gurgling sounds and was clutching at the arrow and scratching frantically at his throat. Lucien looked over the side of the roof to see Arissa looking up smiling. Lucien could feel his face shifting from a returning smile to horror.

Everything slowed as Lucien screamed, "LOOKOUT!"

The warning was much too late as a silver blade burst through Arissa's chest. Her beautiful smile turned to a look of shock.

"NOOOOOO!" Lucien screamed.

He looked as a vampire came from behind Arissa's head to glare up at Lucien. Lucien didn't know how he knew, but he knew this vampire was young and completely insane. The vampire looked up at Lucien and smiled an awful smile, relishing in Lucien's anguish.

The vampire was about to speak when he was suddenly smashed away from Arissa. The blow from Derian's hammer was so powerful that the vampire was sent flying through the wall of the lab like a broken doll. Derian was catching and cradling Arissa before she fell. Lucien couldn't take his eyes from the sword still protruding from the front of her or the blood pooling out of her chest and making its way out her mouth.

"Lucien I have her, you must end this now!" Derian bellowed at him.

The scream of the giant made Lucien regain his thoughts enough to know Derian was right, Zorja wasn't dead, and if the mage got that arrow out, Lucien didn't know how long it would take for the vampire to heal.

With the thoughts of another person he loved dying, the anger of his parents murder, and the pain endured at so many turns to this point, Lucien called on every bit of strength he could muster and pulled. Nothing was happening but he knew he couldn't relent the pressure he had built. He tapped into all the rage and pain he had inside him.

His best friends in his village lying dead, finding the 100 Blades calling card stuck in the door of his home, being captured and sold as a slave, all that he had lost came pouring through his mind and that was turned into more energy and strength. Arissa, only a few feet away, losing her life and him not being able to say goodbye because he couldn't break this stone fueled rage in him he didn't know was there.

His brain flashed all that he would lose if he didn't finish this. His friends and family dying in darkness if he failed. He pulled just a little more. Something tore across both shoulders and down his back. Through the pain he strained, a deep growl came from deep in his throat, his teeth ground against each other, every muscle in his body strained. Then it happened, a small crack gave way to a bigger one, then with one last surge of strength, a huge crack, loud enough for everyone in the vicinity to hear, passed through the air.

Lucien's arms flew apart, then it was as if he was hit by an invisible hand, then the sensation of flying, then…. nothing.

Chapter Twenty

"Arissa!," Lucien screamed as he suddenly sat bolt upright.

A strong hand was placed on his shoulder and a calming voice said, "Easy Lucien."

Master Jerron's kind face came into focus. Lucien took in the fine room and large bed he was in. Master Jerron was seated next to the bed. Confusion was setting in, but Lucien didn't care. He just looked at Master Jerron, tears beginning to fall.

"Arissa," Lucien said softly.

"My boy, she's alive," Master Jerron said.

"What?" Lucien said not wanting to hope. "Master Jerron I saw what happened. She was run through the chest. No human could have survived that," Lucien said.

"Lucien listen to me, there is much to tell. The sword itself sealed its own wound, but you are right even with that she didn't have long," Master Jerron said.

"Then how?" Lucien asked.

"Derian. When the skygem exploded, destroyed once and for all I might add, a mighty force went out and we were at the front of it. You were thrown from the roof, still gripping your blades," the master said pointing to the corner of the room where Lucien's sheathed swords rested.

Master Jerron continued, "Derian shielded Arissa with his own body, and I managed to get a magical shield over Master Mattias and myself. When the force had passed, Derian got the wagon and righted it, all the while cradling Arissa as one would hold an infant. He then got Master Mattias and me into the wagon. Master Mattias was in bad shape but was conscious again. It was then that Derian gently handed Arissa to us. He told us not to remove the sword. She was barely breathing Lucien, a tribute to her will to live. He then picked you up, swords still gripped tight, and put you in the wagon with us. He got his hammer and Arissa's bow and told us to try not to let Arissa move too much, to cushion her as best we could. Lucien, Derian had three swords sticking out of him. One in an arm, one a leg, and one in his side. I told him and he looked at his body as if he didn't know they were there. He removed them, then he picked up the broken traces of the wagon, and he ran Lucien. He went as fast as he could without too much jostling. He blazed a trail through the retreating lines, the battle was over by then and the armies were falling back to outside the borders of the Nightlands, he found his father's medical tent, took Arissa to him, and Master Stein has tended to her ever since. Derian drove his father's wagon, back to Terramilene, inconsolable. He feels he failed her and you for letting her almost die," Master Jerron said.

"That's just ridiculous. Derian led the attack on the lab. He drew almost all of the vampires that were waiting in that building to himself and slew more than half of them, and by your own account we might all be dead, not just Arissa, if not for him. My brother has a big heart to match his size. I will tell him this when I see him. Please, master, tell me everything. Does Rory live?" Lucien said.

"The prince lives. He led the charge with bravery and honor. The armies fought for hours. The Dracúl, Gregor, found him on the field and he slew Brownie," Master Jerron said.

Air went out from Lucien's lungs. It was well known that unicorn and rider bonded heart, spirit, and mind. Tears fell from his eyes for his friend's loss. "Please go on master," Lucien said.

"The two faced off in single combat and the prince fought valiantly and with all he had, but the vampire lord was centuries old and powerful beyond measure. He reigned blow after blow down upon the prince until Rory's shield was crumpled and the prince's arm was broken in three places. No one knows how he was able to sustain that force with a broken arm.

Just when the Dracúl was going to deliver the killing blow, Rob came in and drove his spear through the back of the vampire's knee. Tom came in from the other side and drove his spear down through the armpit of the Dracúl, which pierced his heart. Through sheer will and power the vampire did not instantly turn to dust. The boys screamed at Prince Rory to finish it. With the last of his strength the prince dispatched the Dracúl's head. The battle was pretty much over after that. With his death, and the destruction of the skygem, the vampires lost their will to fight and began retreating to their walled city. The boys got Rory back to the medical tents. The surgeons Master Stein brought from the Citadel of the Mind knew their craft and set the prince's arm and tried to make him comfortable for the trip back to Terramilene. They were also able to…..," the master faded.

"Able to what Master Jerron, please tell me," Lucien pleaded.

"They were able to care for Tom as well," Master Jerron replied.

"What happened to Tom?" Lucien asked, apprehension once again seizing his heart.

"Tom lost an eye Lucien," the master said.

"No," Lucien said his heart breaking for his brother. Lucien was so happy his friends were alive, but he couldn't help feeling grief for the pain they have suffered.

"Each brother blames himself for Tom's injury. Truth be told Tom's taking it very well, he feels the patch makes him look like a handsome rogue," the master said with a chuckle.

Lucien couldn't help but give a small smile at that. But a new realization formed in his mind.

"Wait, Master Jerron you said the twins saved Rory, where was Sergeant Mason?" Lucien said with dread knowing the sergeant would never leave Rory's side.

"You mean the Red Death," Master Jerron said.

"What?" Lucien asked.

"And it's Lieutenant Mason now. This is what General Ravenseye told me. The vampires discovered the location of the general's pavilion and sent an all-out assault on it in hopes to cripple the armies by taking away its leadership. They slaughtered the outer defenses and were getting ready to overrun what was left of the general's personal guard. General Crain and Ravenseye both drew their own weapons and prepared to fight to the end. That's when Sergeant Mason appeared behind the vampires on his unicorn, Stone. The sergeant just smashed into them. He and his unicorn stood alone amongst them, smashing, kicking, hacking, and killing. The sergeant just bellowed his defiance into the vampires that were trying to kill him. Eventually the vampires killed Stone, but the sergeant just rolled free and waded back into the waiting vampires. He had no shield, he lost it in battle, but he did not to care. By that time the sergeant had taken many wounds and blood began to coat his armor. He was like a man possessed and he hit the vampires like a battering ram.

Whatever vampires were left alive in his wake, it was an easy matter for the generals and their men to finish them off with their magically enhanced wooden weapons. The sergeant just kept swinging and bellowing. Limbs went flying. The general told me he saw one vampire sent flying fifteen feet through the air, chest caved in. Another he saw cut clean in half at the waist. And then an eerie silence came over the camp. Mason lost his helm, and he was covered head to toe in blood, much of it his. There were many empty shells of vampire armor and many laying around wounded. They were dispatched by the generals and their men. The sergeant just stood there breathing heavily, eyes scanning, looking for more enemies to slay.

The generals knew that was a dangerous moment, the sergeant might still be in his own battle madness and could just as easily kill anyone who came near him. Both generals spoke calmly and quietly to him as they both drew near and put their hands on his shoulders lightly. The sergeant finally looked at them and recognition entered his eyes. Then the madness was broken and at that same moment the sergeant collapsed. The generals ordered some men to get him to the medical tents for immediate attention. General Ravenseye told me that he and General Crain were saddened because he saved them, and they didn't think he would survive his wounds. The sergeant slew or disabled 30 vampires during their assault. Who knows how many he killed before that."

Lucien shook his head in disbelief. He understood how Derian could accomplish such a feat but a single human to confront and slay that many vampires was more than he could comprehend.

"They wanted the men to return with a report on the good sergeant. Two of the four men they sent returned and reported to the generals that the Lady Lucretia intercepted them in her own wagon and told them to put Sergeant Mason in the back of her wagon and that he was under her care. The men told her they had their orders to take him to the medical tents at which point she looked at all four men and the look she gave them had them fear for their lives. They put him in the back of her wagon and then ordered two of the soldiers to stand watch and make sure she was not disturbed. General Ravenseye convinced General Crain to let the situation go, that Sergeant Mason couldn't be in better hands," Master Jerron said.

"She loves him doesn't she?" Lucien asked.

Master Jerron took a moment before answering, "I have known the Lady Lucretia for a long time. She suffered a loss in her life which has led to her being exactly what most see, a hard, cold, stern, but beautiful woman who rarely ever smiles. To see her care for and about Sergeant Mason makes me very happy. It makes me believe that those walls of pain she built around her heart are starting to crumble. She deserves some happiness."

The master came out of his moment of thoughtfulness and continued, "Anyway, as soon as the Lady Lucretia allowed it, the generals went to him, thanked him, and promoted him to lieutenant. Of course, the sergeant felt he didn't deserve the promotion for letting himself be carried away from the prince's side during the battle. I've never seen so many people willing to take on guilt for things that they could never control."

"Quinn and William. Timber and Benagar?" Lucien asked next.

"Your cousins are fine. They have a few scars each which Quinn could not be prouder of," Master Jerron said.

"Wait, you mean the rear guard was needed to fight?" Lucien asked.

"Oh yes. The vampires set a trap and routed the archers. They would have been completely massacred and the army would have been beset from in front and behind if not for Prince William leading the rear guard into battle. They saved many lives. As far as Timber and Benagar, I swear adventuring with you, and now taking part in this battle, those two old wolves have gotten younger. That fire that they were known for so long ago has been reignited in them. Your cousin was right to ask for his command. All the tension and hard pride that he has grown up with seems to have melted away. He already smiles more now, and you can catch a glimpse of the king he will one day become," Master Jerron said.

Lucien looked to the ceiling and smiled in thankfulness that his friends and family were all alive and that they would heal. Happy that he was still alive to help them heal, to be there for them as they have always been there for him. Lucien started to get out of bed when Master Jerron put his hand on Lucien's chest.

"I know you wish to see everyone but please bear with me a moment more. I want to prepare you for when you see Arissa. She has instruments in and attached to her. Dr.

Stein had everything he needed brought here to Castle Brightstone knowing her healing would be better served surrounded by everyone who loves her. Dr. Stein hasn't slept in over a week. Derian said this was not beyond his father's limits but it's getting close. As far as everyone else, their injuries and scars are easily seen, but there are some that cannot be seen. You have all been through and seen so much horror. You have always been stronger together. I know that if you continue to do so, and lean on each other as you always have, you will all get through this as well. Now Lucien I want you to tell me how you feel physically, humor me," Master Jerron asked when Lucien gave the master a confused look at this new question.

Lucien took a moment. He didn't feel any pain. He actually felt pretty good, strong. He inhaled deeply and smelled food cooking. This made him realize he was very hungry.

"I feel very good master. Very strong. I am quite hungry. Other than that, fine," Lucien replied.

"Alright then grab a robe and slippers and we'll go see everyone and get you some food," Master Jerron said.

Lucien went over to where the robe and slippers were. There was a full-length mirror there as well and when Lucien saw himself he froze in place. His hair was now silver. Not grey or white but silver. There was a gleam to it that the sunlight in the room reflected. His eyebrows were silver. Everywhere on his body that there was hair was now silver.

Master Jerron appeared in the mirror behind him, "They are calling you the Silverwolf reborn."

"Master…I…how?" Lucien stammered.

"I have a theory which we will talk about with your family. For now, I have kept you too long. Come, let's go see everyone. They have all taken turns sitting with you and the longer you slept the more their worry grew."

Lucien put on the robe and slippers and exited his room with Master Jerron close behind, and joy in his heart.

Chapter Twenty-One

Lucien entered the hallway and instantly recognized where he was, Castle Brightstone. It was the same wing he and his friends stayed in when they visited. A few rooms down, sitting on the floor, back against the wall, head down, was Derian. As Lucien grew closer he could tell Derian was sleeping. He hated waking his friend, but he had to speak with him.

"Derian," Lucien said while giving his friend's arm a shake.

"Hm, what? Lucien!" Derian said sleepily at first then springing up and gathering Lucien in for a huge embrace.

"You're awake!," Derian exclaimed.

"So are you," Lucien said with a laugh.

"How are you feeling?" Derian asked.

"I'm fine Derian. How are you doing my friend?" Lucien asked with sincere concern in his voice.

Derian's face changed from joy to pain and shame. It broke Lucien's heart.

Derian looked at the door he was sitting outside of, "Lucien, I'm sorry."

"For what Derian. For saving all our lives, including Arissa's. You forget Master Jerron and I were both there. He told me everything you did after the skygem was destroyed. We were all there and none of us kept Arissa from getting hurt. Did you wish to protect her any more than any of us did?" Lucien asked.

"Lucien it was so close. So close to losing her," Derian said.

"But we didn't. That is because of you. Let go of this pain Derian. No one looks at you as anything else but the hero you are," Lucien said.

The pain in Derian's face eased and he embraced his friend again.

"Bah! I told you the same thing days earlier young man. How come when he says it does it finally gets through?" Master Jerron asked annoyed.

"You're not the Silverwolf reborn," Derian replied to Master Jerron with a smile.

Lucien sighed heavily, "She's behind that door isn't she?"

"Lucien, my father is in there with her, and even though she will live, her condition is delicate. My father hasn't slept, and he's barely eaten. What he's doing…..I'll let him explain," Derian said as he knocked gently on the door.

Master Stein opened the door slightly and smiled as he saw who was waiting outside. He came out of the room and shut the door behind him. As he turned Lucien embraced him quickly.

"Thank you so much Master Stein. I can't even think of my life without her. Because of you and your son I won't have to," Lucien said.

"You are very welcome my boy. I've become very fond of all of you. I wasn't about to let anything, let alone a battle with vampires, take *any* of you from me. I'm selfish that way," Master Stein said with a smile.

"Can I see her?" Lucien asked.

"Lucien, we must talk. I'm sure Master Jerron told you some of what to expect. She *will* live Lucien, I assure you, but to look at her now you may not believe it. She is resting deeply now. The truth is she is asleep far more than she is awake. Rest is essential to her healing," Master Stein said.

"I understand Master Stein," Lucien replied.

"Lucien there is something else," Master Stein started, "Arissa truly was at death's door. I've never seen a wound so grave, and anyone survive it. Her will to live is strong. Because of the severity of her injury, I had to begin the process of altering her Lucien," Master Stein said.

"What do you mean?" Lucien asked.

"Basically, I had to begin the process of making her, well, like me. The alterations I have done to myself to slow down aging and to make myself a better, more efficient, human being physically, I had to begin in Arissa. It was the only way to save her. I assure you," Master Stein said.

"Are you telling me that not only is Arissa going to live, but she will live with me throughout the centuries. That I won't lose her to time?" Lucien asked.

"Well essentially yes…OOF," Master Stein said as Lucien crushed him in another embrace. The thought that he would outlive Arissa by centuries came to his mind once, but he banished this thought quickly. Their love was so new, and they were still so young he would not let this thought darken them and what they had, but this news from Master Stein was almost too joyous to bear.

"I understand your joy Lucien but for right now you must trust me. The process will take months. Right now, she needs rest. When she gets stronger you may see her. Give it two more weeks and she will be strong enough to receive visitors," Master Stein explained.

"I'll absolutely follow what you say Master Stein. Will you do something for me? Get some sleep. Eat something. You must be reaching even your limits. We're going to get something to eat, please come with us. Arissa needs you at your best," Lucien said.

"Well, I suppose I could use a little of both. Arissa is resting now, and I was only writing notes in my medical journals on the findings and updates to this point," Master Stein replied.

The four went downstairs, making their way toward the kitchen area when they walked into Prince Rory, his left arm casted and in a sling, but otherwise looking as strong as ever. Lucien's cousin, Brienne, had her arm through his right arm. The twins had their usual smiles on their faces. Tom had a patch over his left eye with a hint of a scar above and below it. Lucien was overjoyed to see his friends, but it pained his heart to see them hurt.

"Lucien!" Brienne shouted as she gently removed herself from Rory. She ran to him, threw her arms around his neck and kissed him on the cheek. She then struck him in the arm and said, "It's about time you woke up. We've been worried, despite Master Jerron's assurances. Your hair is beautiful Lucien," Brienne said.

"Thank you cousin," Lucien said.

"Yes the Silverwolf reborn!" Tom said loudly.

"Oh look at his face! He looks almost as uncomfortable with us calling him that as Rory does when we call him prince," Rob said.

"I thought he was pretty before but now with that hair he may truly be beautiful," Rory added with a smile.

Brienne leaned up and whispered in Lucien's ear, "Go to your brothers but be mindful of Rory's arm."

Lucien nodded but he could hold back no more and closed the distance quickly. He embraced the twins first.

"Welcome back brother," the twins whispered in each of Lucien's ears.

Lucien leaned back to look at them both, he started to say something to Tom.

"Don't say a word Lucien. I can see that look on your face. You want to try to take blame for this," Tom pointed to the patch over his eye, "my brother and I *chose* to fight, not just with you, but for everyone. The thought of a vampire horde sweeping over our home, well there really was no choice," Tom said.

"I was just going to say that you *do* look like a handsome rogue with that patch," Lucien said with a smile.

"I do, don't I," Tom said smiling, raising his chin and puffing out his chest.

Lucien then turned to Rory and embraced his friend gently being mindful of his arm and being under the watchful eye of his cousin Brienne.

"Rory… I am so sorry about Brownie. My heart breaks for you brother," Lucien said to his friend.

"When it happened, I didn't have time to feel it, but I've had plenty of time since to mourn him. It's like a piece of me is gone. There will be many new bonds formed. I wasn't the only one to lose a friend. Many unicorn and rider connections were broken. Enough of that though. I have mourned enough and can again later. Right now, I am far too happy to see you up and about, brand new hair just gleaming in the sunlight," Rory said with open sarcasm.

"Wait… Master Jerron you didn't tell me about Master Mattias. Is he alright?" Lucien asked ashamed he just now thought of him.

"Master Mattias is recovering. His injuries are not of the physical kind, he's healed from those. Master Mattias is in fine physical condition for a human his age. In the battle with the vampire mage, even with the two of us combined, the vampire was far more powerful. Master Mattias gave everything he had, called upon every ounce of magical strength that he could. Because of that strain on him there is but a spark of magic left in him. I've been with him; we have spoken at length. He will live. Some mages just fade away and die if the magic is suddenly gone. Tragically some take their own lives. Master Mattias is just struggling with feeling like he is now useless. The king and queen have assured him that they have no thoughts of replacing him, reminding him that through his years of service they have rarely needed his magic. They've needed his wise council far more, and they are sure he has plenty of that left. He just needs a little time of self-reflection to adjust to his new state of being," Master Jerron said.

"I'm glad he's alright. I just wish he hadn't lost so…OOOF!" Lucien found himself lifted in the air and looking down into the smiling face of his cousin Quinn.

"Ha! Back among us finally. You've slept long enough cousin." Quinn asked playfully.

Quinn put Lucien down and then crushed him in a strong embrace.

"So, Quinn I hear you've picked up some scars you're proud of," Lucien said.

"Bah! Mere scratches. I've learned something about scars though…. girls love them. Oh, they fawn over you and want to know the stories behind them," Quinn said.

"Our cousin doesn't have to worry about that brother, he already has a girl, one of the strongest any of us will ever meet," William said with a smile.

"Well said brother. She'll be back with us in no time, back to putting me in my place with a clever comment or a raise of an eyebrow," Quinn said with a smile.

William and Lucien embraced.

"So, William how does it feel to be a hero?" Lucien asked.

"I can't lie, it feels pretty good. I can see why you all enjoy it," William replied.

Lucien noticed the change in William, as if a cloud had lifted from him. He seemed more at ease, more confident and at peace with himself. Lucien was glad that someone came back from the battle with something more than just pain, loss, scars, and bad memories.

"You saved many lives William and brought much honor to the Farrunner name," Lucien said.

"Thank you Lucien," William replied smiling.

"There they are Sera. Somehow they just find each other," King Killian said as he and Queen Sera joined them from a nearby corridor.

"How could they not Killian they are bound together by so much," Queen Sera replied.

They quickly made their way to Lucien. The queen hugged him first in that way that reminded Lucien so much of his mother. There was so much love in it.

"How are you Lucien? How do you feel?" Queen Sera asked.

"I feel good Aunt Sera, a little hungry," Lucien replied.

"Arissa will be back with us soon enough Lucien," the queen said.

"That girl is stronger than us all I should think," King Killian said.

Lucien then found himself engulfed by his uncle.

"Perhaps if you can ignore your hunger for a little while longer we can all eat together a proper meal," said King Willem who had just joined them with Queen Gwendolyn.

"Your hair is magnificent Lucien," the queen said.

"The queen's hair still outshines all," Lucien replied.

"Charmer," the queen said with a smile.

"Welcome back Lucien. You destroyed the skygem. All of Arborreah owes you their thanks," King Willem said as he shook Lucien's hand.

"The king is too kind. If there are thanks to be given, many are deserving. I couldn't have succeeded without the sacrifice of so many. I would have been killed by the vampire mage if not for…Arissa," Lucien ended that sentence in almost a whisper.

King Killian stepped in front of Lucien until Lucien met his uncle's eyes.

"You take heart Lucien. She is under Dr. Stein's care and there is no one better. Be patient," Killian said.

"Of course, uncle you're right," Lucien said.

"My pride for you all knows no bounds. Your parents would be proud of you as well Lucien," King Killian said.

"Thank you uncle. William is greatly changed and for the better. He walks taller but with more ease," Lucien said changing the subject.

"Yes, he was right to ask for his command. I would have kept from it. He is already proving to be a wiser king than I," King Killian said face beaming with pride as he looked at his eldest son.

"Oh, I don't know about that uncle, after all you did give him his command. In the end you listened and trusted him. Be careful uncle, you keep doing things like that and you're going to relinquish your title of *stubborn old wolf,*" Lucien said with a big grin.

Everyone had a good laugh at that. When the laughter subsided, King Willem spoke.

"Alright how about we meet in the royal dining room in two hours. That should be plenty of time to freshen up for dinner."

As everyone began going to their rooms, Master Jerron called out, "Lucien, Quinn, can I see you both for a moment?"

The boys came over and said, "Yes Master Jerron."

"I'd like you boys to do me a favor as you come to dinner later," Master Jerron said.

"Sure, master what is it?" Quinn asked.

Two hours later everyone began making their way to the royal dining room. Lucien and Quinn were dressed in robes and slippers, and they were carrying the mirror from Lucien's room. Master Jerron came over to them and told them to put the mirror in the corner until after dinner. As the boys were walking to their seats they were intercepted by Brienne.

"Why are you two dressed like that and why have you brought that mirror?!" she said in a scolding whisper.

"Easy sister, this is Master Jerron's doing. He wanted us to dress like this and bring the mirror. Supposedly we'll find out why after dinner," Quinn said.

Everyone was there with a few additions. Lieutenant-Colonel Mason, who was indeed promoted again after returning to the castle, and the Lady Lucretia were there. Lieutenant-Colonel Mason looked as strong as ever, but Lucien could see the Lady Lucretia watching him closely and doting on him. Master Mattias was in attendance. He walked slowly and looked as if he had aged twenty years, but he still had a spark in his eye and a smile on his face. There were places set out on the table for Timber and Benagar who would be eating with them instead of taking up their usual positions behind the king. There was an empty seat and place setting which puzzled Lucien. Derian sat at the end of the table with his father. Derian had to sit on the floor. The king assured Derian that like King Killian he had craftsmen hard at work making furnishings for his size. General Ravenseye had taken the army of the Great Wood days ago. He sent by raven word to King Killian that the army received a hero's welcome by the people. The people were slightly disappointed the royal family would not be returning yet but were quickly alright with it when they realized all this meant was there would be at least two welcome home celebrations.

With everyone seated and the wine poured, King Willem with his glass in hand, "I know everyone is hungry, so I'll make this short. Our families are blessed, you all returned to us, when so many did not. In two days, I will address the people to mourn our losses and acknowledge our victory. There will be tales told and songs sung about the heroes of this battle, so many in this very room, but the pride we feel is nothing compared to the relief we feel at your return to us. That empty place setting is for Arissa who will soon be joining us, but until then, and as always has a place with us. So …. To family," King Willem said as he raised his glass.

"To family," everyone replied.

The servants brought out the courses and it wasn't long before the table was full of food. Lucien and many others at the table ate like they hadn't eaten in a week. Healing brings on an appetite, and the fact that they were mostly all together, brought back the will to eat more. The conversation was lively and joyous, full of laughter. When everyone was done eating Master Jerron stood.

"I know you've all been wondering why I had these boys, forgive me, you've all been through, and done too much to be considered boys any longer. I had these young men dress in robes and bring down that mirror for a reason. I would like to conduct an experiment. Lucien, Quinn please get the mirror and bring it over," Master Jerron said.

The boys did as they were asked and joined Master Jerron close to, but still away from the dinner table.

"Bear with me as I give you all a lesson on magic. To larger or smaller degrees magic flows through everything, rocks, trees, grass, mountains, the wind, everything. Living things are no different. Werewolves, humans, unicorns, the faraway griffons, and yes, vampires. This is my theory as to what happened to Lucien when the skygem was destroyed. The original Lucien Silverwolf struck the skygem while it was activated and spewing darkness into the sky. The histories are specific about the gem imploding first before there was an outward force that we thought destroyed the skygem. While Lucien Silverwolf was killed I believe the implosive magic of the skygem drew in the magical aspects of him, and yes maybe some of his spirit. Now when *our* Lucien destroyed the skygem, I believe in that instant of explosion, that the magical aspects of the original Silverwolf, drawn to our Lucien's uniqueness, entered Lucien, and that perhaps the spirit of the original is what protected Lucien from death. After all Lucien you were standing directly in front of the skygem when it was destroyed, you shouldn't have survived," Master Jerron said.

"So, what does it all mean Master Jerron?" Lucien asked.

"Maybe just a hair color change, but maybe something more. Lucien I want you to assume the forms," Master Jerron said.

"Master Jerron you know I cannot. I wouldn't even know how," Lucien said, the old shame in his voice.

Master Jerron lifted Lucien's chin and not gently, a fire in his eyes, "There will be no more of that. You have brought honor to yourself and your family. You have done too much in service to the realms for you to feel shame over something you were born with and have no control over," Master Jerron said sternly but with love behind his words.

"Well said!" both kings shouted in unison after which the whole table echoed their sentiment.

"Very well Master Jerron what would you have me do?" Lucien asked with a smile.

"First prepare yourself. Use your techniques you learned at the citadel. Specifically focus and fighting through and blocking out pain. When werewolves are born they will change shape on instinct and the first few changes are painful, until finally the changes come with ease. None of us even remember those first painful changes. You are a young man attempting this for the first time, if you are successful, I am sorry Lucien, but you will feel great pain. Do you still wish to try?" Master Jerron asked.

"I do master just tell me how," Lucien replied.

"Alright when you have your focus ready and your mind clear, call upon the power of the wolf. Let it flow through you while picturing yourself in second form. When the pain comes you must push through until the change is complete. Do you understand?" Master Jerron asked.

"Yes master," Lucien said.

"Alright then. Prepare yourself and when you are ready, begin," Master Jerron said as he stepped back.

Lucien took a deep breath. He looked over at his unusually quiet cousin Quinn. They met eyes and Quinn nodded, waves of excitement and anticipation came off of him and everyone else in the room. Lucien took off his robe and stepped out of his slippers. The humans, not nearly as comfortable with nude bodies in public, averted their eyes. Lucien focused his mind, called upon the power of the wolf, and thought of himself in second form. The instant he formed that image, pain hit him. Waves of pain from the inside out. It was overwhelming but he held the image in his mind and fought the pain. He heard screaming and realized it was him. He heard voices filled with concern. Quinn started towards him, but Master Jerron ordered him and everyone else to stay back.

Lucien's bones were breaking and mending, his skin was stretching to the point where he thought it would split. Silver hair was sprouting out all over his body. He felt his face stretch into a snout. His screams turned to howls. Guards burst into the room, and he heard King Willem tell them that everything was fine and to return to their posts. Then the pain started to subside. Lucien began to straighten his back and he realized how much taller he was now. He was a little wobbly but he was quickly adjusting.

When he came in for dinner the room was candlelit, but now it was as if the sun was out and fully lit the room. His sense of smell was incredible, he was almost overwhelmed by it. He clenched his hands and felt impossibly strong. He heard and understood everyone speaking. He heard Master Jerron tell Quinn to change. Lucien watched his cousin disrobe and then change to second form. His cousin changed form with fluid ease, and he was still much bigger. Then wonders upon wonders he heard Quinn asking him if he was alright, but he heard him in his mind! Lucien went to answer, but on instinct he tried to speak, but his mouth would no longer form speech and all he heard was some strange yips and barks come from his mouth. He heard Quinn laughing in his mind.

"Cousin just answer me with your thoughts. I'll teach you about verbal communication later. Look at yourself cousin, look in the mirror," Quinn said.

Lucien turned to the mirror. He had to duck down a little bit because he was now too tall to fit within the mirror. The sight of himself stunned him. Shining silver fur was everywhere. His eyes shone blue. He looked at his ears and wiggled them. He went to smile but all that happened was his lips pulled back into a fearsome snarl.

"Many new sensations to get used to Lucien. Lean on your family and me and we will tell you everything you need to know about your new forms. We will help you adjust. Now do you think you are up to trying for third form?" Master Jerron asked.

Lucien tried to think *yes* to Master Jerron, but the master gave no indication he heard him.

"First lesson cousin. While in the wolf forms the thought-speak doesn't work with a wolf in first form. Just nod," Quinn said.

"Thank you cousin." Lucien thought back.

Lucien looked at Master Jerron and nodded.

"Excellent! Now just do what you did before but now picture yourself in third form," Master Jerron said.

Lucien calmed his mind and thought of himself in third form. Again, the pain was immediate as his body broke and re-shaped itself. He found himself dropping to all fours. He watched as his hands re-formed into massive paws. He felt the odd sensation of his tail growing. He howled his pain until it began to subside. He opened his eyes; he wasn't as tall as he was in second form, but he was more massive. He felt the muscles and power that this form possessed. He looked over at Quinn who was also in third form as well. The power of this form was incredible! The smells were even more overwhelming in this form. He shook his head to try and clear it when he heard his cousin in his head.

"It's the smells isn't it?" Quinn thought.

"Yes," Lucien thought back.

"Don't worry cousin. I will be there to help you through it all. How to separate smells and not be overwhelmed. For now, take a look in the mirror," Quinn thought.

Lucien turned to the mirror and was stunned yet again. His form was too large width-wise this time to see all of it in the mirror but he saw enough. Gleaming silver fur and piercing blue eyes. There was a stunned silence in the room until he heard Master Stein say, "Magnificent." He heard clapping and the twins started shouting, "Silverwolf! Silverwolf!" which others in the room took up. When the clapping and cheering subsided Master Jerron stepped up to him.

"Amazing Lucien. Just amazing. Now back to first form," he said.

Lucien pictured himself in human form and the pain came. It still hurt very much but the transformation was less painful than the others. When he transformed back Master Jerron handed Lucien and Quinn their robes and slippers. As soon as he put them on he was surrounded by his family. The outpouring of joy from them all was incredible. He had always wanted this, the ability to assume the forms, and he was overjoyed that he was now able to, but a thought entered his mind about something he might've lost. He quickly put the thought from his mind, hoping his face didn't show it. Everyone was so happy he didn't want to ruin the moment.

Lucien was about to turn in for the night when he heard a soft knock at his door.

"Aunt Sera what a surprise. Please come in, is everything alright?" Lucien asked.

"Well, that's why I'm here Lucien, to make sure everything is all right with *you*," she said.

"What do you mean?" Lucien asked.

"When you finished your transformations and everyone was celebrating with you, I saw a flash of sadness cross your face. You got rid of it quickly, but not before I saw it. May I guess as to why that look crossed your face?" Aunt Sera asked.

"Yes," Lucien answered quietly somehow knowing his aunt's guess would be correct.

"You were thinking that now that you are a full werewolf you were no longer half human, and you were feeling the loss of that human side. That somehow you were losing your mother," Sera said.

Lucien could only nod, the emotion was too raw for speech. His eyes began to go blurry as tears formed. He missed his mother so much in these quiet times, especially if his aunt Sera was near, as she shared many of the same qualities.

"Oh Lucien did these physical changes you've gone through affect your heart or memories? No, your mother will always be a part of you. Nothing can change that. You had no choice in being half-blood and no choice now in being full werewolf. You have lost much Lucien, but don't lose sight of what you've gained. So long as you remember her you will keep her in your heart and she will *never* be lost," his Aunt Sera said.

Lucien embraced his aunt, "I wish you could have known her," he said.

"So do I. Whenever you wish to talk about her, I will always listen," his aunt said as she kissed his forehead.

His aunt turned to leave but she turned back once more and said, "Lucien I can never take your mother's place, nor would I ever presume to, but I want you to know that I love you like you were my own son," and with that his aunt left his room.

Lucien closed the door behind her smiling as he happily realized that his wise aunt was right and that he was foolish to ever think he could lose the part of him that was his mother. She lived in his heart and mind and always would. He fell asleep thinking of her with joy in his heart.

Chapter Twenty-Two

Wounds, both physical and mental, healed over the next few weeks. Some better and quicker than others, like what happens with any war. The young men, and women, who returned from the battle with the vampires leaned on their family and friends to help them regain their strength. No one could recall what day it was, but eventually the city regained its buzz, its exuberance that made Terramilene the greatest city in all of Arborreah.

During that time, King Willem addressed the people of Terramilene, recounting the great victory over the vampire lords and the destruction of the skygem. He acknowledged the heroes of the battle, both those who returned and those who were lost. Medals, awards, and promotions were given to those who distinguished themselves. He told the people that, as always, the two great nations, the Great Wood and Terramilene, stood together and triumphed together. Tales of heroism spread through the city and songs were being written and sung at inns and gatherings each day and night.

King Killian, Queen Sera, and Prince William returned to the Great Wood. Their people needed to hear from them. A similar address of heroism was given to the werewolves. The king and queen beamed with pride when the heroism of Prince William was told and the voices of the people of the Great Wood may have been heard back in Terramilene.

The king told the people about Arissa and her situation and how Lucien would not leave her side while she healed. It was also shared how Prince Quinn would not leave Lucien's side as his cousin cared too much to let him sit through the situation alone. There was also news that Princess Brienne stayed in Terramilene to look after Prince Rory as he healed, and the subtlety of that statement was not lost on the wolves of the Great Wood. He told them that once Arissa was healed, fully, that the rest of the family, which included the Steins would make their way home. The people understood and looked forward to *that* celebration as well.

That night, all the wolves of the Great Wood ran through the woods until they got to the Crag of the Moon and cried out their howls for all those wolves who lost their lives in battle. It was not until almost daybreak before they returned to their homes. Being tired, and exhausted from the strain of emotions, took its toll on the entire kingdom but they were happy to do it as they gave a proper send off to those they would never see again while walking amongst the Great Wood.

Arissa healed and got strong enough to where she could receive visitors and be showered with love. Lucien filled her in on everything. He gave her his uncle, aunts, and cousin William's apology for not being there when she awoke, but the demands of a kingdom never rest. Lucien stated they looked forward to seeing her soon though. Arissa was overjoyed that everyone in their small group had survived the battle but was saddened by the pain they had endured. She was amazed and delighted by the changes in Lucien and couldn't wait to ride with him in third form.

Arissa told both Derian and Master Stein how grateful she was for the parts they played in saving her life. Hearing Arissa say this finally allowed Derian to let go of any feelings of guilt he had left. Dr. Stein explained to her that she had more procedures to go through, but they would get easier the stronger she became. He told her that when these procedures were done, she would be like him. Greatly improved physically and that she would live for centuries. She was a little overwhelmed by this news at first, but once she realized that she and Lucien could grow old together, she hugged Master Stein as tightly as she could and thanked him again.

Derian spent time between helping his father care for Arissa and training with the Hammeraxe Legion. He was determined to become a better fighter. To learn every nuance of heavy weapon fighting from the best in all of Arborreah. He was dedicated and disciplined, and his skills improved quickly.

Prince Rory's arm healed and was soon as strong as ever. He and Lieutenant-Colonel Mason had much work to do with recruiting and training new potential members for the Legion. New unicorns had to be found and bonds made for all the Legionnaires who lost their steeds. Rory and Mason also had to find new unicorns and form new bonds. It was a difficulty Rory had accepting, but knew it was a responsibility he could not avoid. Everyone knew that his next unicorn would never hold the same place in Rory's heart the way Brownie did.

Lucien, the twins, and Quinn spent much of their time outside the city walls training. Quinn taught Lucien what it meant to be a werewolf. He helped Lucien adjust to his new power. How to pick out and differentiate between smells. How not to be overwhelmed by all the new feelings and sensations he was going through. The transformations became less and less painful. Soon he would feel no pain at all shifting between forms.

Lucien noticed the twins trained harder than he'd ever seen them train. They were refining their technique to adjust to Tom's blind spot. Rob vowed they would be even better than before. Lucien didn't doubt it. A few more years of training like they were, and they may become unbeatable.

The weeks were good ones full of healing of body and spirit. Then, a day of sadness. The twins announced it was time for them to go home. Everyone knew the day would come, but it hit everyone hard. King Willem and Queen Gwendolyn insisted the boys stay a few more days so a raven could be sent to the Great Wood to inform King Killian and Queen Sera. This would allow a proper goodbye for everyone. The boys agreed, knowing it would be rude to refuse and because they would like to see King William and Queen Sera and Prince William one more time before they left.

Those last few days were spent together with Lucien, Arissa, Rory, Brienne, Quinn, and Derian, sharing meals together, laughing, and telling stories. King and Queen Farrunner arrived but without Prince William. The king apologized to the boys as it was his decision that William stay behind and sit on the throne to get a feel of running a kingdom, at least for a few days. King Killian told them how disappointed he was and to tell them that the prince was going to miss them greatly. The boys understood and told the king and queen that William was going to be a great king someday.

After an early dinner on the last day before the twins were set to depart, the group went to the lounge area, got a fire going, got a few bottles of wine, and spent their last moments together. Day turned to night, and no one wanted to go to sleep, to let their last day end. The servants found all of them the next day passed out in the lounge area. The fire had gone out and all the wine bottles were empty. If a more perfect setting for friends could be found it would be hard to be believed.

It was the break of dawn and after awakening everyone the servants told them to quickly freshen up and make their way to the eastern gate by order of the king to give the twins a proper send-off. The group quickly did so. They splashed cold water on their faces, straightened their hair, and changed clothes with all due speed, not wanting to keep those waiting at the eastern gate for long. They met at the steps of the castle leading to the street. The twins had their packs and their staves, and the group realized that this truly was happening. Their group that had been together for so long was ending.

The streets were mostly empty as the city was still waking, but there were those who saw the royalty and hero group and easily recognized them. Cries of *Hail Prince Rory* and *Hail Silverwolf* would flow up the street to them. When the group reached the street leading to the eastern gate, it was lined on both sides with soldiers in gleaming armor. As the group, the twins in the lead, walked the streets the soldiers began thumping the bottom of their spears on the ground creating a rhythm. They finally reached the gate where a large contingent of people were waiting for them. The soldiers stopped their spear thumping in unison. Arissa, Lucien, Rory, Brienne, Quinn, and Derian stepped away from the twins as they said their goodbyes.

First was Master Jerron who had never left Terramilene but spent his time with Master Stein exchanging ideas as their friendship grew. Master Jerron embraced them both and wished them safe travels.

Next came Master Stein. "Master Stein, we can never tell you enough how grateful we are to you for saving Arissa," Rob said.

"Allow me to return that gratitude boys. The way you have accepted my son, his life has never been better and that is in large part because of you two and the rest of your amazing companions. Safe travels boys," Master Stein said as he embraced the twins.

They then stood before Timber and Benagar. "It has been an honor to share the road with you and to fight next to you," Timber said with Benagar nodding in agreement. Timber and Benagar extended their hands to be shook, but the twins stepped up and gave them large bear hugs instead. The two old warriors laughed and returned the embrace.

They moved on to Lieutenant-Colonel Mason.

Tom took a deep breath, "Lieutenant-Colonel Graham Mason. My brother and I have learned so much from your example. How to be better soldiers and men. Thank you for everything."

"Please take care of him m'lady," Rob said to Lady Lucretia, who stood behind Graham, watching over him. She returned the statement from Rob with a nod and a smile.

"Boys, I have not met many men in my life with more honor, loyalty, and bravery, than you two. Your parents will be very proud, as I am. Safe travels," Lieutenant-Colonel Mason said as he and the twins exchanged embraces.

The boys then stood before the kings and queens of two of the most powerful kingdoms in all of Arborreah. The emotions the boys felt almost overwhelmed them. These four people treated them like family when they were far away from their own, and they loved them for it.

Queen Sera stepped forward first. She hugged the boys and kissed their cheeks. She looked up at them, tears falling. "I feel like two of my sons are leaving me. You boys are family now and there will always be a place for you in our kingdom and our hearts."

The boys smiled and nodded as their own tears fell. Emotion robbing them of speech. King Killian was next. He took the boys in his big arms and squeezed them tight. He released them and looked into their eyes.

"You followed Lucien because of friendship and loyalty. You risked your lives with my son and watched over each other. You fought selflessly in a battle you didn't have to fight in. Willing to sacrifice all for the sake of others. Friendship, loyalty, selflessness. If I knew nothing else, these things would be enough," King Killian said with a big smile on his face and pride in his voice.

"Thank you King Killian, Queen Sera," the twins said in unison through the emotion in their voices.

Finally, the boys stood before King Willem and Queen Gwendolyn.

The king spoke, "These wagons have many items for you both and your family. You will find you sheriff license, new farming tools, and the clothes from Terrance's. The queen also had clothes for your brothers, sisters, and parents packed into the wagons. There is more than enough gold to get a proper sheriff's office up and running. I've sent a ravener, with ravens, so communication between us all won't take so long. He will teach you how to use them and care for them properly. Four members of the Legion will escort you and act as criers when you get back to your community. Your people need to know, no, *must know*, what you have done for everyone. Though, I am sure the travelling minstrels and storytellers will probably have told your town by now. The horses you claimed from the Shadowmen are waiting for you and the wagons and the horses pulling those wagons are yours as well."

"The king is far too generous, but thank you very much," the boys said.

"That's funny, I was just telling the king that I didn't think it was enough. The truth is boys it will never be enough. The two of you saved our only son," Queen Gwendolyn said.

"He would have done the same for either of us. He is our brother," Rob said.

"Yes, you are his brothers which is why you will always be thought of as our sons," the queen said. She kissed both boys on the cheeks and as they began to pull away she laid a small leather pouch into each of their hands.

The queen whispered, "for the road, if you find some things you'd like to buy, you deserve it." Later the twins would look in the pouches to find it filled with many gold coins.

The king embraced both boys and wished them safe travels.

The boys looked at both royal couples and said, "Thank you all for everything." Then they walked over to where their friends were waiting. Before they reached them Brienne rushed up to them.

"I wanted to say goodbye first. You both deserve time to say proper goodbyes with those you have spent so much time with. When Lucien came back to us I knew I had gained a cousin. What I did not know was that I was also gaining two more brothers and a sister. I miss you already. Safe travels," Brienne said as she engulfed the two boys in a hug.

"We miss you already too Brienne, and we are very happy about you and Rory. There couldn't be a more perfect match," the boys said as Brienne went and joined her parents.

The twins came before their friends. They went to Derian first.

"Derian, my brother and I have been talking, and we know why you are so big. A smaller person would never be able to contain your heart," Tom said as he and Rob were lifted from the ground in Derian's embrace.

"This is not goodbye little brothers, only, until we meet again. Safe travels," Derian replied.

Quinn was next. He crushed them both in the hug that only Quinn could give.

"I can't believe you are both leaving me. Now the burden of laughing, joking, and fun for this group falls solely on my shoulders," Quinn said jokingly, but then his face grew sad, "I'm going to miss you brothers," he said.

"Don't worry Quinn, when you all come to visit us we'll throw a party that will more than make up for all the fun we've missed," Rob said.

The boys then walked over to where Arissa, Rory, and Lucien waited.

"That's right as soon as I'm done with all of Dr. Stein's procedures and healed, we're coming to visit," Arissa said.

"You make sure you do exactly what Master Stein says. Don't rush things. We'll be waiting in Hollister," Rob said.

"We've been through so much together. I love you both so much. Please be safe," Arissa said.

"We will little sister. We love you too," Rob and Tom said. They gave her careful hugs and kissed her on her forehead.

They then stood before Rory and Lucien. The four young men embraced each other tightly. Rob spoke first.

"Rory, I know Tom and I teased you a bit with *Prince this* and *Prince that*. The truth is you were our brother before you were our prince. After you went back to being Prince Rory, you were just as you were as our brother. Kind and generous and always there when needed. You are everything a true prince and brother should be."

"I went to the citadel to train and hoped to make some real friends. I never imagined I would gain three brothers and a sister. The two of you are everything a friend and brother should be. I will miss you two making me laugh. Lieutenant-Colonel Mason is a fine soldier and mentor but not too much for laughing. I love you brothers and I will miss you," Rory said.

The boys turned to Lucien where Tom spoke, "Lucien you were the first example to us of real-life heroic honor. You lost so much and in the face of daunting odds you avenged that loss. You kept your word to Master Stein. You always do the right thing no matter what the consequences may be. How could Rob and I *not* follow you anywhere? You would be there for us; how could we not be there for you?"

"You know what I've always been amazed at with you two? It's the fact that you two have been just as heroic and brave and loyal as any of us. Your names are in the stories and the songs being sung, and none of it affects you. You both are still who you are: twin brothers from the town of Hollister far to the east in the farmlands. You set out to graduate from the citadel and get a sheriff's license. You have done that and so much more. You left your town boys and now return as living heroes. Your family and your community will be as proud of you as I am. I love you Rob. I love you Tom. Thank you for everything. Safe travels until we meet again," Lucien said.

The boys mounted their horses, turned to everyone with smiles and tears on their faces. They said together as twins sometimes will," We love you all. Until we meet again."

With that the boys and their procession started out of the eastern gate. People had gathered to watch them leave. A chant of "Hollis" was taken up to send the boys off with a hero's goodbye.

Everyone missed the twins more and more with each step the horses took the brothers away from the castle. It was a new phase the companions would have to work through, and life doesn't allow anything to stay the same, no matter how close you are to someone.

Epilogue

Mort enjoyed the cool waters of his grotto on this warm night. One of the many luxuries of the manse he now owned and lived in. With more wealth than he could ever spend in three lifetimes, thanks to his vampire masters, it was easy enough to move into the more affluent area of Terramilene under the guise of a wealthy trader. No more long nights on the road in filthy inns, in filthy towns. Now, he was to spy on a better class of people. Everything in his life was about the best of the best. He especially enjoyed the scantily clad woman who fed him grapes. He was very pleased at the doors that opened with the wealth he had, and the women who would keep him company.

The girl let out a shriek of fear. Mort was instantly alert and had his hand on the dagger that was hidden under a nearby towel. A man in a long black cloak was standing to the right of Mort. He was tall and broad-shouldered, but the hood hid his features. As if he could read Mort's thoughts the man reached up and took the hood down.

"Royce?" Mort said.

"Hello Mort," Jackson Royce replied.

Mort took his hand off of the dagger underneath the towel. This was the Cobra, one of the deadliest men alive, and Mort was not. He decided his best course of action would be to listen to the intruder, for now.

"How did you get in here?" Mort asked.

"It really wasn't difficult Mort. Oh, don't blame your guards they were merely outnumbered and really had no choice but to let us in," Royce said.

"Us?" Mort asked. He quickly looked around the room and noticed someone else with them. He was standing in the shadows to the left of Mort. He was wearing a long green robe with a deep hood that hid his face.

"Don't worry none of them are dead. They are being watched over until after we've had our conversation. As a matter of fact, my dear, this conversation is not for your ears," Royce said.

The Cobra held out his hand to the young woman to help her exit the pool. He handed her a towel to dry off and said, "Please wait in the master bedroom, I'll be along shortly to apprise you of what's going on. Don't worry, no harm will come to you," Royce said. When the girl left he turned back to Mort.

"How are you even here Royce? Last I heard you were waiting to be hanged," Mort asked.

"Very true. I was, but fortune smiled on me again and as it turned out I had information that the two great kings of Arborreah needed. I traded that information for a full pardon of ALL past crimes and my freedom. They deemed in their wisdom that my information was indeed valuable and both King Cromwell and King Farrunner honored our agreement and granted me my pardon and my freedom," Royce said.

"Alright so what are you doing here? Who is this with you? Are you here on behalf of our vampire masters?" Mort asked.

"Hmph," Royce chuckled.

"The vampires have bigger problems to worry about after their defeat in the Battle of the Nightlands as it is being called. My sincere doubt is you will ever hear from them again. As far as why I am here and who my companion is, that would be due to the second deal I made with the two great kings. A deal of a more personal nature. You see, King Farrunner has a nephew. I'm sure you know who he is as his name is on everyone's lips. He is part of the group that the people are calling the *Young Heroes*," Royce said as he swept an arm towards the figure in the shadows.

The man stepped forward into the light and removed the hood from his head to reveal long silver hair. Of course, Mort knew who this was, this young man and his companions fame was growing by the day, the silver hair was just the confirmation. The newcomer looked at Mort as if he were nothing. No emotion showed on Lucien Farrunner's face, just an empty coldness behind his piercing blue eyes.

"I don't understand," Mort said.

"Allow me to further enlighten you. The information I traded was the identity of the man who killed young Lucien's grandparents on his mother's side," Royce said.

A cold sickness began to form in Mort's belly as things became clear.

"Yes Mort, Lucien never even got to meet his grandparents, you took that from him. Then you gave the information the vampire lords needed to find him, and because of that his parents and entire village was killed. What did I receive in return for this information? All that you have Mort," Royce said as he turned around in a circle, arms outstretched.

"You're no better than me Cobra!" Mort shouted at Jackson Royce.

"Your hands are dripping with as much, if not more, blood than mine," Mort said.

"You're right Mort. I'm not any better, just luckier. There was something else to this second deal though. I am now in the service of the good kings of Arborreah, and I know that no matter how much good I may accomplish in their service, my hands will never be completely clean. But a man can hope to be better, can't he? Ah well I've taken up enough time talking. I have to see to your, well, my guards and that lovely young lady and tell them about the change in management. Goodbye Mort," Royce said and then left Mort alone in the room with Lucien.

Mort looked over at the young man who was now disrobing and transforming.

"Please no…." Mort pled.

The last thing Mort saw was eyes that were blacker than a moonless night, silver hair, then fangs, then nothing.

Made in United States
North Haven, CT
10 November 2022

26543643R00143